SPECIAL DELIVERY

Other Nick Polo Adventures by Jerry Kennealy

Green with Envy
Polo's Wild Card
Polo in the Rough
Polo's Ponies
Polo, Anyone?
Polo Solo

SPECIAL DELIVERY

A CASE FOR NICK POLO

■

JERRY KENNEALY

■

ST. MARTIN'S PRESS
NEW YORK

PRODUCTION EDITOR: SUZANNE MAGIDA
PRODUCTION MANAGER: KATHY FINK
DESIGN BY DAWN NILES

Library of Congress Cataloging-in-Publication Data

Kennealy, Jerry.
    Special delivery / Jerry Kennealy.
        p.   cm.
    ISBN 0-312-08304-1
    I. Title.
PS3561.E4246S67   1992
813'.54—dc20   92-27464
                                                    CIP

First Edition: December 1992

10 9 8 7 6 5 4 3 2 1

This book is dedicated to my aunt, Grace Kennealy

1
.

"No problem," said Raymond Singh for what must have been the tenth time.

"But Ray," I protested, "I've never been to London. I wouldn't know my way around. I'd get lost over there."

"No problem," he repeated. "Hire a guide."

We were interrupted by a small, wiry guy with parchment-colored skin who must have been in his seventies. He pointed a gnarled finger at the rack of liquor bottles behind the cash register and in a croaking voice said, "Walker, red."

Singh dutifully pulled a half-pint of the Scotch whisky from the rack and slid it across the counter to the gentleman, who had neatly piled the exact amount of money needed for the purchase in front of him. Singh scooped up the paper and coins and dropped them onto the cash register, without bothering to ring up the sale.

"See you later, Tony," Singh said to the man's retreating back. He glanced at the digital watch on his wrist and said: "That'll last him till this afternoon. Then he'll be back for another bottle."

While I was at the counter trying to convince Raymond

Singh that I was not the man he should hire for the job he wanted done, at least a half-dozen people had come in, all much like the man who purchased the Johnny Walker scotch: elderly, poorly dressed, an air of gloom hanging over their heads. All had ordered a pack of cigarettes and half-pints of liquor. "Mickeys," we used to call them when I was a kid. I didn't know they sold half-pints anymore. All the requests had been for top-of-the-line hooch: Beefeaters gin, Stolichnaya vodka, Jack Daniels whiskey. "Why doesn't he just buy a fifth or a quart and not bother coming back this afternoon?" I asked Singh.

He turned his sad hound-dog eyes on me. They were brown, the color of coffee that had stayed on the stove all night. He had changed a little since I'd seen him last, maybe put on a few pounds, and while his hair was still oil-slick black, his neatly trimmed beard showed streaks of white, like lighting flashes against a dark sky.

"If he were to buy a fifth or a quart, he would have to share it," Singh explained. "Or he would have it stolen. With a half-pint he can safely keep it in his pocket and nip away." The dark eyes turned glassy. "I wrote to the tobacco companies, the major labels—Philip Morris, Camel, Marlboro, Virginia Slims, all of them—and suggested that they make a package of just five or ten cigarettes, not twenty. I could sell a lot more cigarettes if they came in small quantities like that. A full pack of cigarettes makes you a marked man in this area. Everyone wants to bum one off of you. If I could—"

We were interrupted again, this time by a woman, who could have been anywhere from fifty to seventy, bundled up in a tattered black coat, her gray hair half covered by a bright green bandanna. She gave Singh a big smile, showing an uneven row of yellowing teeth. "Black Jack," she said in a voice already slurred by alcohol. Singh exchanged a mickey of Jack Daniels for a crumpled five-dollar bill, dropping the change in the woman's shaking hand.

The next customer was young, nervous-looking, his hands constantly rubbing down the front of his leather jacket. Singh's eyes turned hard. He adjusted his corduroy pants, the back of which had slid down, revealing the top of his jockey shorts. The black plastic checkered grip of an automatic pistol stuck out of his back pocket. He made sure the customer got a glimpse of the gun. The young man paid for his two candy bars and hurried out. "He looked like trouble, didn't he?" Singh asked.

I nodded in agreement. One of the mysteries of life was why Raymond Singh bothered working the counter of the mom-and-pop minisupermarket in the tenderloin district. I hadn't checked on his financial background lately, but the last time I did Singh was the listed owner of no less than sixteen pieces of real estate, and that was just in San Francisco. He had other properties in the Bay Area. He also owned a title company, a restaurant, and a half-dozen more mom-and-pop places scattered around town. But this was where he had gotten his start, his "flagship," as he liked to call it.

Singh had come to San Francisco from the slums of Calcutta some twenty years ago. He had adapted quickly to the American way of life. He had worked hard and hustled his way up the social and financial ladders of life. He was a big political contributor to many Democratic Party causes. There was no sense in contributing to Republican causes in San Francisco. There are more women priests in the Vatican than there are Republicans in the city of Saint Francis.

A few years back, when I was a member in good standing of the San Francisco Police Department, working homicide, Raymond Singh had been the prime suspect in the murder of another East Indian wheeler-dealer. All the evidence pointed his way. His lie-detector test had been inconclusive. He had hooked those hound-dog eyes of his onto me like searchlights following a stripper across the stage, pleading his innocence, like they all do. But something about Singh rang true. As I dug deeper into the case it was obvious that he wasn't the guilty party. Any detective handling the case would have come to the same conclusion, but he felt as if I were his personal savior. When he was released and the actual murderer, a transient from Florida, was arrested, Singh began showing up at my doorstep with cases of Dom Pérignon and boxes of Havana cigars.

Even after I left the department the gifts kept coming. Even after I made a stupid mistake and ended up in a federal prison for six months, Singh kept sending his thank-you gifts. Do you have any idea what an eight-inch Monte Cristo Cuban cigar will buy you in prison? A pack of cigarettes is worth killing for, to some yardbirds. The cigars helped buy me what I needed most: to be left alone.

A slim, dark-haired girl, barely out of her teens, wearing tight Levi's and a tank top with the words "Dos Equis" stretched to the breaking point across her chest, came and relieved Raymond of his cash-register chores.

I followed Singh to the back of the store, past rows of canned food, boxes of cereal, and a small, understocked produce stand, through a pair of swinging doors, to a warehouse stacked to the ceiling with cardboard boxes, most bearing liquor labels, and finally into his office, a long, narrow room stacked with yet more liquor cases.

Singh settled behind his desk, which sat on a platform some two feet high. The top of of the desk was littered with three telephones, a fax machine, an answering machine, two Rolodexes, and an assemblage of business papers strewn about haphazardly, entirely covering the desktop from one end to the other. Against one wall was a Hewlett Packard computer. Right next to that was a printer and a small copying machine. The far wall had a two-way mirror that gave an excellent view of the store's cash register.

Singh went to the window and gazed at the young girl behind the counter, shaking his head. "My niece. She's been here in this country for only a year, but unfortunately she acts like she was born here. You know what I like most about Regina's Levi's?" he asked. From my view the answer was rather obvious.

Singh chuckled. "If she stole a dime and put it in those pants, I could tell if it was heads or tails." He pulled open a desk drawer and drew out a box of cigars. "Help yourself, Nick."

I took a cigar and ran it under my nose. Singh took one for himself and toasted the end with a heavy gold Dunhill lighter. He held the lighter out to me. "I'll save it for after dinner."

Singh went back to his desk drawer and dug up another box of cigars. "Take them, Nick." I held up my hands in protest.

"Raymond, one cigar is fine. Thank you. Now let's get back to business. I can't go to London for you."

"Why not?" he asked, sinking slowly into the black leather office chair.

"I don't know the town, Raymond. You want someone to do a job for you, get someone who knows the territory."

Singh worked the cigar thoughtfully from one side of his mouth to the other. "No problem. I told you. Hire a guide. I need someone I can trust."

"What the hell do you need done in London, Ray?"

"A delivery. I want you to deliver a package to someone."

I winced and shook my head. "Ray, I'm not going to play—"

"It's just a letter," Singh said in a hurried tone, his hand searching among the rubble on his desk. "Here it is. Nothing funny, Nick. Just a letter, a check, and a tape. That's all. Look."

It was a normal-sized business envelope, unsealed. Inside was a piece of folded white paper, a check, and a microcassette tape. I looked at the check first. It was a cashier's check, made out to a Gurbeep Singh. The amount was for sixty thousand dollars. I looked down at Raymond Singh. "Gurbeep?"

He did a movement with his hand that looked like he was the pope blessing the multitudes. "A cousin. A distant cousin," Singh said, the emphasis heavy on the "distant." "He prefers being called Gordy."

I looked at the letter. It was handwritten in ink, in a language I couldn't recognize.

Raymond Singh's hands were busy moving papers on his desk. Buried under there somewhere was a small player-recorder. He gestured with his fingers for the microcassette in the envelope, slotted it into the machine, and pushed the play button.

The voices were of two men. One sounded like Raymond Singh. Again the language was foreign, spoken rapidly by both parties. No shouting, no harsh words. They could have been discussing the weather or, for all I knew, the assembling instructions for an atomic bomb.

"That is a conversation between Gordy and me, in Hindi,

5

the language of my country. A business transaction. You give him the envelope with the tape, the letter, and the check." I got the full force of one of Raymond's smiles, all sweet innocence and sincerity. "It will be no problem, Nick, believe me." He scribbled something on a piece of paper. "Here, you can reach me at this number when you've made the delivery."

"Do you know where your cousin is, in London?"

"He owns a shop. I have the address." More digging through the refuse on his desk. This time he came up with a standard-sized color photograph. "That is Gordy," Raymond said. "His address is on the back."

The picture showed Raymond Singh with his arm around a man, both of them smiling into the camera lens. They were wearing business suits, white shirts, quiet ties. Gurbeep was an inch or so shorter than Raymond, at least twenty pounds lighter. He had a full head of black hair, combed straight back from his forehead, and a small mustache under a rather prominent nose.

"There are a lot of people who could look like this guy, Raymond. I'd hate to hand over a check for sixty thousand dollars to the wrong man."

Again he came at me with the "no problem." He pulled up his shirt and the yellowing white T-shirt underneath it, and ran a hand up his belly, stopping when it got to his left breast. He circled the nipple with the nail on his right index finger, hard enough to leave a red mark against the olive skin. "Gordy has a scar, right here. Almost a full circle. If you have any doubts, make him show it to you to prove it is he."

I tried to get out of it gracefully. "This time of year the flights to London are probably booked solid."

"No problem," Singh said, taking the cassette from the machine and handing it to me.

"I'm going to have to drop what I'm working on. It will cost you a small fortune to send me over there."

Singh reached back into a desk drawer, pulling out a pile of bills held together by a thick red rubber band. "No problem," he echoed, tossing the money my way.

I put the money in one hand, the envelope with the letter, tape, and check in the other, balancing them as if on an assayer's scale. The pile of money was heavier, but somehow my hands came to rest at an even keel.

"I'm not sure whether my passport is valid," I said.

Singh's head snapped up and he blinked his eyes rapidly. "That could be a problem."

2

■

I recently read an article in the Sunday paper whose author was trying to make the point that the ever-popular middle class was catching up with the rich. The writer said that things that only the super-rich could afford just twenty years ago are now easily available to almost everyone. For instance, years ago only rich movie producers had small theaters in their homes where they could project black-and-white eight-millimeter prints of last year's movies. Now you can slip a color, stereo-recorded Hollywood feature into your four-head video recorder a few months after the picture is released. So-called midsized economy cars now have standard automatic transmissions, air conditioning, power windows, and cassette and compact-disc players. Even exotic, out-of-season foods that the super-rich had imported at great expense can now be found in most supermarkets. Maybe so, but if you want to know where the old cliché "rich is better" comes into full play, compare flying economy to first class. The pale-gray leather chair squished nicely when I wiggled against it. I stretched my legs out to their full length, luxuriating in all the room around me. I had an aisle seat, with just one window seat to my left. My flying companion was a serious, rather nerdy-looking chap in his mid-thirties, thin-faced, with lank, straw-colored hair that continually fell over his forehead and had to be brushed back. Round-lensed, horn-rimmed glasses were pushed down to the end of his straight nose as he peered at the laptop computer set on the seat-tray in front of him. The cabin steward had hung up his expensive-looking pinstripe suit coat, so he sat there in his white-on-white shirt, paisley tie, and bright-red suspenders, pecking away at his laptop computer. The obligatory Cartier tank watch was on one wrist. A gold fountain pen and black leather notebook lay on the tray next to his computer. All in all, an expensive-looking package, but somehow I got the feeling that scruffy old Raymond Singh could have bought and sold him several times over.

Raymond had certainly bought me. A check of my seldom-used passport showed that it had a couple of years of travel time left. While I had protested long and loudly to Singh about the trip, I was really rather excited. I took a sidelong peek at the computer, which was filled with columns of numbers. My traveling companion tilted his head slightly my way, wrinkled his face in a way that caused his glasses to slide farther down his nose, and swiveled the screen out of my sight.

"Harmmmmmph," I said, which was the same reply he'd given me when I'd introduced myself right after takeoff. Then I stretched out my legs again, raised the glass—real glass—of iced Russian vodka to my lips, and gave a silent salute to the poor folks back there squeezed into the sardine-can seating of the economy section, scrunched together with barely enough elbow room to maneuver their plastic knives and forks over their trays of tiny portions of cold chicken, while drinking domestic wine out of plastic cups, then finding out once the movie started that they'd been positioned behind a bald-headed former basketball player.

First-class chow was duck pâte, asparagus salad, medallions of veal with herb sauce, calabrian noodles, and Baba au rhum with strawberries, washed down with Moët et Chandon champagne served by a lovely and generous stewardess. Any arguments about rich being better?

I was about to ask for another order of dessert when the

stewardess informed me that breakfast was only a few hours away, so I spent the rest of the trip intermittently dozing, poring over the maps and tour guides of London that I'd picked up at the airport, and trying to convince myself that the trip was going to be a simple matter of getting off the plane, taxiing to the hotel, working off the jet lag, finding good old Gurbeep Singh, delivering Raymond's envelope, then spending a few days in town as a sightseer.

The packet of money Raymond Singh had shoved my way contained five thousand dollars in American money and another thousand in British hundred-pound notes. "Keep track of all your expenses," Raymond had crooned into my greedy ear. "They will be paid when you return."

"No problem," I had volleyed back to him.

I took out the envelope to be delivered by hand to Gurbeep Singh. I had had Raymond make me a copy of the check, then watched closely as he sealed the envelope. There were no switches, nothing else inserted, just the cashier's check, the handwritten letter, and the microcassette tape. The player-recorder was packed away in my luggage. What the hell did the letter say? What had old Gurbeep done that he was to be awarded with a cashier's check for sixty thousand dollars?

Why pay me a small fortune to deliver it? Why not just wire him the money? I asked myself. Because it involved something illegal? Raymond Singh was no monk, but I couldn't see him mixed up in anything like smuggling or the drug trade. So the money could be a payoff, or the down payment on some property Raymond wanted to buy in London, or a bribe for past or upcoming favors, or a gambling debt. It could be a lot of things, none of them my concern. I was just a mailman, a very well paid mailman.

No problem, I told myself, repeating Raymond's favorite phrase. Most of me listened, but not my stomach, which was a little queasy. I hoped that was the result of the baba au rhum.

Another advantage of flying first class was that you were off the plane seconds after it docked at the terminal. Customs had no interest at all in my one piece of carry-on luggage. The bored

11

official asked the purpose of my visit, not bothering to glance up when I said, "Business."

My first sight of London was of a gray sky that looked exactly the same pewter shade that had been hovering over San Francisco ten hours earlier. It was time to play tourist, hop into one of those lovely, old-fashioned, high-topped cabs that Alec Guinness and Jack Hawkins used in the movies. The backseat was big enough for five people and their luggage. The cabby asked me a question, which, after I said "Huh?" a few times, I finally deciphered as "Where to, guv?"

Raymond Singh's travel agent had booked me into the Ritz. Who was I to argue? I gave him my destination and he took off with a grunt.

I tried starting a conversation several times. He was a sociable enough chap who, when learning this was my first trip to London, started pointing out landmarks to me.

You know the old joke about the American tourist getting into an argument with a hotel clerk? The American says: "Where's the elevator?"

The Clerk says: "The lift is back there, sir."

American: "I asked for the elevator."

Clerk: "The lift is back there, sir."

American: "They're called elevators, buddy."

Clerk: "Lifts, sir."

American: "Well, we invented the damn things, and we call them elevators!"

Clerk: "Yes, sir. But we invented the language. The lifts are back there."

They may have invented it, but for all the good my driver's travelogue was doing me, I could have been listening to Raymond Singh's tape.

One part of the conversation came through loud and clear when we pulled up to the Ritz Hotel. "Twenty-eight pounds six, sir," he said in an intonation with all the clarity of Richard Burton doing Hamlet.

Close to sixty bucks for a cab ride. Singh's expense account or not, I vowed to take the underground back to the airport on the way home.

After the passing of more pound notes to the doorman and the uniformed bellman, who led me through a baroque lobby dripping with gilt chandeliers and gold-leaf-trimmed mirrors, I found myself in a spacious suite with an antique brass bed and a massive marble fireplace with real firewood stacked neatly in front of it. The window looked out on a view of a misty-green park.

I showered, drying off with a deep-pile royal-blue towel that must have weighed a couple of pounds. I tried taking a quick nap, but so far jet lag had passed me by. The advice given by travel-weary friends was to forget about jet lag and just get onto business. If it's midnight where you land, act like it's midnight and go to bed, even if you've had a full night's sleep on the plane.

The ornate clock on the fireplace mantel showed that it was just 4:30 in the afternoon. I adjusted the Timex on my wrist, spread out a multicolored map of London on the bed, and tried to get my bearings.

According to Raymond Singh, his distant cousin Gurbeep's shop was located on Carnaby Street, in the Soho area. According to my map and tour guide, the Ritz was located in Saint James's. Maps were never one of my strong points, but after no more than five minutes I'd found the Ritz, very near Saint James's Park, where all those high-level MI5 and MI6 characters from Deighton and Le Carré novels met to plot out their next moves in the never-ending quest for those damn Russian moles. Carnaby Street seemed to be a mile or so north of the hotel. It was time to breathe in some of that foggy London air. I made sure I had Raymond Singh's envelope and put the copy of the check into one of the Ritz's blue envelopes, which was so thick it felt like cloth rather than paper.

There was no fog, just dusty, concrete-filled air. Every building in London seemed to be either undergoing reconstruction or getting a cleaning job. I trooped along with the well-dressed tourists carrying expensive-looking shopping bags down Piccadilly Street to Regent Street.

According to my map, I was now at Piccadilly Circus, which looked more like a small, comparatively neater version of Times Square. The animals looked much more friendly then their New

13

York counterparts. I was getting a tourist's stiff neck from ogling all the architecture. Even what were apparently just office buildings or shops had a definite flair: sweeping balconies, beautiful brick-and-wrought-iron trim. They were little jewel boxes that would all have been stamped untouchable landmarks in San Francisco in hopes of holding off the ball-and-crane boys, who appeared set to start plans for demolition as soon as the fresh concrete had dried on the latest addition to the skyline.

Carnaby Street was just a couple of blocks long, taken up with small shops under ancient, two-story brick buildings, the majority of the shops specializing in flashy-looking garments, the windows filled with studded leather jackets, skirts, and garter belts, Union Jack–emblazoned men's underwear, acid-head sweatshirts, and all manner of whips, chains, and handcuffs.

Gurbeep ("Gordy") Singh's place had the name BeeJay's stenciled over the front entrance. The smell of leather was almost overpowering. I weaved my way through racks of khaki jackets, pants, vests, and exotic undergarments in wild floral colors. The merchandise looked like a combination of Banana Republic and Frederick's of Hollywood. The music system was turned up to ear-hemorrhaging volume. A nasal voice kept chanting the lyric "I want to pull your tits" over and over, no doubt one of those long-lost Gershwin melodies recently discovered in a dusty trunk at a Broadway theater.

The clerk behind the counter was a redhead-brunette chap in his twenties. The left side of his head was carrot-red, the right side the color those Grecian Formula TV models end up with after a few weeks' use. "And no one at the office noticed the difference!" His face was chalky-white. A vein on his neck throbbed in seeming rhythm with the music. A plastic tag on his black leather vest bore the name Ronnie.

"Is Gordy in?" I shouted into his right ear, hoping my notes would get through the tangle of gold earrings.

"Uhhh?" he asked.

"Gordy. Gurbeep. Mr. Singh. You know, the owner."

"Gordy?"

"Yeah." I made a gesture of writing on the palm of my hand. "The guy who pays you, signs your checks."

14

"Oh. Gordy. He ain't in, mate."

"When will he be back?"

"You an American?"

"Right."

"I'm gonna get there one day. Soon. Get out of this shit-hole."

"Don't blame you," I said, knowing that he'd have no trouble finding employment in Uncle Sam land. He'd been born to be a clerk at Tower Records. "What about Gordy?"

"He ain't in."

"When will he be in?" I shouted, just as the song ended.

"Who knows? He's the boss. Comes in when he wants to."

I took out the envelope with the copy of the certified check, scribbled a note—"Call me at the Ritz Hotel"—on one of my business cards, slipped the card into the envelope, sealed it, and handed it to Ronnie.

"See that Gordy gets this. It's very important, worth a lot of money to him."

Ronnie nodded his head and tossed the envelope casually toward the cash register. "Will do, mate. Will do."

3
.

Just a few years ago there were hundreds of "safe" telephone booths in San Francisco. Now there are barely a half-
dozen that I know of, and unfortunately they're not long for the
world. Nice, big, quiet booths where you can go in, close the
door behind you, and be reasonably sure that no one, even the
person in the booth right next to you, could hear your conversation. There are often times in my line of work when you need
that privacy, when you're reporting to your client or asking for
confidential information. Or when you may be using a pretext
and you can turn on your little tape recorder with the special-
effects tape in it, the booth suddenly booming with the sounds
of an office full of typewriters clacking and printers printing, so
the person you're talking to may get the impression that he is
actually speaking to a police officer, or a postal inspector, or a
newspaper reporter. Times when it just wouldn't do for the guy
in the booth next to you to tap you on the shoulder and inter-
rupt your spiel with a stupid question such as "Hey, buddy, you
really with the FBI?"

A friendly tip, if you happen to use any kind of cellular
mobile phone: Be careful! Anyone can walk into an electronic

17

store and purchase a broadband RF scanner and bug right into your conversation. Or a simple modification on their own cellular phone to the same frequency you happen to be broadcasting on and they lock right onto your conversations. Of course, the eavesdropper is playing hit and miss this way. He may get you, or he may get anyone who happens to be on line. If the eavesdropper knows what he's doing, and he really wants you and you alone, he simply plays around until he gets your cellular electronic serial number. Every time a cellular customer dials a number the serial code is transmitted first, so the phone company knows whom to bill for the call. Once smarty pants has your number he can use a cellular service monitor, once again an item sold at your friendly electronic store for repairing cellular phones, interface it with a personal computer, and zoom right in on your code. Bingo, he's got you anytime you send or receive a call.

Obviously this is all illegal, and our watchdog members of Congress, knowing this, passed something called the Privacy Act of 1986, which strictly prohibits the interception and monitoring of cellular telephone conversations. Anyone caught doing so faces "criminal penalties." Impressive. Intimidating. However, there has never been one single arrest made in the United States under the statute.

Ah, but London. They know how to make a phone booth. Big, beautiful monsters of brightly painted red cast iron and glass. If we had them in the States the homeless would make condominiums of them. Drug dealers would put in desks and fax machines. Hookers would upholster them in black leather and chains.

I fiddled around in my pocket, found a coin that fit in the phone's slot, and dialed information. No listing for a Gurbeep or Gordy, or even G. Singh.

I got the number for BeeJay's and good old Ronnie answered the phone. I used my best Gunga Din voice and asked for Mr. Singh.

"Not here," Ronnie barked over the screeches of a rock guitar.

"When will he be back?" I asked politely.

18

"Later. Maybe in the morning."

"Do you have a number where he can be reached?" I asked a disconnected phone. Ronnie had hung up, no doubt to jack up the stereo's volume.

It was time to start spending some of Raymond Singh's expense money. Not knowing a soul in London, I did it the hard way, let my fingers walk through the yellow pages. There were eight pages of listings under "Detective Agencies." One of them actually had the nerve to feature a sketch of a Sherlock Holmes type smoking a pipe and holding a magnifying glass. I settled on an ad that claimed the gentleman had been in business for twenty years and had "extensive Scotland Yard experience." If he had been around that long he was either reliable or crafty enough not to get his fingers caught in some legal cookie jar.

"Proctor Investigations," a man answered in a clear, modulated tone. We were off to a good start. At least I could understand him.

I introduced myself, gave him my credentials, and told him just what I was after. "The man's name is Singh. First name Gurbeep."

"Are you joking?" Mr. Proctor inquired.

"No. Goes by the name Gordy. Operates a shop called BeeJay's on Carnaby Street. I want a home address for him and a list of any properties he owns."

"Ah, yes. I see. Can I ask just why you're interested in Mr. Singh, sir?"

"I have some papers I want to give him."

"Ah. We do process-serving, Mr. Polo. Reasonable rates."

"Personal papers, Mr. Proctor. I just want a home address. No big deal." And it wasn't a big deal. Back in San Francisco I could have pulled the information off my computer in a matter of minutes. But here I was the proverbial fish out of water, at the mercy of the local sharks. "Look, Proctor. If you're too busy and can't handle it I'll call someone else."

"Ah, we can fit you in, I'm sure. About billing, sir."

"I can give you a check or cash. I'm staying at the Ritz."

That seemed to perk up his interest. "The Ritz, you say?"

"Yes."

19

"I don't think there will be any problem, Mr. Polo. When do you need the information?"

"Soon as possible."

"Ah, yes, that—"

"I'll pay for rush service. But remember, I'm in the business. I know what it takes. And besides, maybe someday you'll need some work done in San Francisco and I can reciprocate."

Proctor's mumblings showed that he thought that was not a very strong possibility. "Should have the information for you by morning, noon at the latest. You say you can pay in cash?"

"As long as you give me a receipt."

"That will be no problem," Proctor said, causing the hairs on the back of my neck to send shivering signals down my spine. "I'll drop by the Ritz with the information. Maybe we can have lunch."

"Enjoying your stay in London, Mr. Polo?" George Proctor asked, sipping his wine with small, dainty swallowing sounds, then licking his lips.

I knew I had made a mistake picking Proctor the moment I saw him. He was in his mid-fifties. "Portly" is the way I guess the British would describe his build. A shade over six feet in height. What was left of his hair was gray. A thick mustache sat under a pitted nose finely netted with broken blood vessels.

It was his clothes that worried me. The dark-blue suit was well cut. The thickness of his starched, white broadcloth shirt showed that it had not been purchased ready-made. The heavy, silk-rep tie probably represented some school he'd attended or some regiment he'd served in. Even his shoes looked tailored, black leather shined to a gloss so bright you could use it as a shaving mirror.

Expensive was what he looked. Expensive was what he was when I checked the envelope he'd handed me. A bill for a hundred and eighty pounds and a single one-page report showing that "investigative checks under the names Gurbeep/Gordy Singh proved negative."

"Nice town," I said, tapping the bill on the edge of the tablecloth. We were sitting in the Palm Court, in the lobby of the

20

Ritz Hotel. I had mistakenly wandered down in slacks and a sweater, only to be told by a distinguished, well-groomed man that there was a strict dress code. "Even for guests, sir," he had explained patiently in a tone he worked hard on to keep the superiority from showing through. So I had padded back up to my room and put on a tie, Mervyn's, class of Christmas 1989, and my by now rather overtraveled-in blue blazer.

"Expensive," I added, looking from his bill into his eyes.

He was used to complaints. Didn't even blink before saying: "Yes, very. Didn't turn up much on your chap, Singh. Are you sure that's the right spelling?"

"Positive. What about the store, BeeJay's? Couldn't you pull any information out of there?"

The waiter hovered over us, asking if we were ready to order yet. Proctor certainly was. He ordered smoked salmon glazed with a peppercorn-and-pink-champagne sauce, salad, and asparagus tips. "Marvelous fish here," he proclaimed. "Marvelous."

Proctor's bill had spoiled my appetite. "Just eggs, over easy, and wheat toast," I told the unimpressed waiter.

Proctor pulled an alligator-leather notebook from his suit pocket. "Thought you might be interested in that," he said, donning a pair of Benjamin Franklin glasses as he flipped through the notebook pages. "Licensed under the name Carlisle, Inc. Address same as the store."

"What about personal names?" I asked. "There has to be somebody listed."

"Yes. Right you are." He went back to his notebook, obviously reluctant to release the information in front of his nose. "A Marta Howard. Again same address as the store, on Carnaby Street." He smiled warmly and dollar signs grew in his irises. "Want me to run a check on her?"

"Not right now, thanks."

Proctor was the persistent type. "Don't happen to have a photograph of your man Gurbeep, do you?"

I passed him the picture that Raymond Singh had given me. "The man on the left is Gurbeep Singh."

Proctor studied the picture, then cautiously looked over

21

both shoulders. If he expected to see anything but large, potted palm trees, gilded statues, and pink velvet chairs filled with well-dressed, matronly women, he was going to be sorely disappointed. "Bloody wogs all look alike, don't they?" Proctor said in a soft, confidential voice.

"Do they?" I reached for the picture.

Proctor gave me a nervous smile. He looked a little confused, worried that he may have made a slip of the tongue. For all he knew I could be married to a "bloody wog." He took a swallow of his wine. "If you need a surveillance on him at the store, I've got a couple of men free."

He might have a couple of men, but George Proctor didn't give anything away free. "I'll think about it."

I showed poor American manners by wolfing my food down and signaling for the bill before Proctor could get his mitts onto the dessert cart. After signing the restaurant bill, I wrote out a check to Proctor for the amount shown on his invoice.

"I thought you said something about cash, old boy," he said, wiping up the last of the fish sauce with a piece of bread.

"I did. But that was before I knew you were going to give me a royal British screwing."

The last word came out much louder than I had intended, causing the three ladies at the table directly alongside ours to stop, like a freeze-frame, with loaded forks traveling toward their lips.

"Here, now," Proctor protested, "there's no need to—"

"No need to screw me. You did about fifteen minutes of work, all on the phone, and charged me close to four hundred American dollars. I don't mind getting seduced," I said, standing up and bending close to Proctor's ear, "but I hate to be raped." Screwed, seduced, and raped. The ladies would certainly have something to talk about over tea.

4
.

I went back to my room and checked the phone directory under Carlisle, Inc. No listing. Proctor had dangled the company's name under my nose like bait on a hook. Once I was on that hook, he'd charge another few hundred dollars for a few minutes' work. As long as I was throwing Raymond Singh's money around, I might as well give it to my regular sources.

The long-distance operator led me by the hand through the intricacies of international dialing, and within minutes I was connected to Raymond Singh's office in San Francisco. Raymond was nowhere to be found. I next called my money guru in Southern California, who didn't appear at all impressed by the fact that I was calling from the Ritz Hotel in London.

"What do you want, Polo?" he asked in that grumpy, uninterested way of his. From what little I knew of him, and I didn't want to know any more, he had once been a federal or state bank inspector. He combined his former contacts with a master's degree in computer hacking and could pull up financial data on anybody. One rumor I'd picked up was that he had been hired by the staffs of both the Republican and Democratic candidates for governor of California to dig up all the dirt he could find on the opposition. Of course the party on the left didn't know he was also working for the party on the right. He'd found some interesting and embarrassing material on the Democrat's wealthy spouse, which many claimed made the difference in a very tight race.

"Can you get information on a company here in London?"

"Certainly," he said matter-of-factly. "Can you afford to pay the extra charges?"

"Certainly," I said with the confidence that playing with other people's money gives you. I gave him the Carlisle, Inc., name. "A Gurbeep Singh or Marta Howard may be the owners. Anything you can find on Mr. Singh would be appreciated."

"Two days," he said.

"I'll pay for rush service."

"Twenty-four hours, Polo. Price doubles."

"No problem," I said, mimicking my client.

I rubber-necked my way back down to Carnaby Street. The headlines in the newspapers spoke of hard economic times, but you couldn't tell it by the throngs of shoppers and sightseers. Carnaby Street was elbow to elbow with an eclectic mixture of skinheads in leather, a young crowd wearing everything from American-football-team sweatshirts to camel-hair topcoats, and a swarm of camera-toting tourists.

BeeJay's had its fill of customers. Rapid Ronnie was behind the counter working. I used my favorite phone booth again. Ronnie was all business this afternoon.

"Mr. Singh isn't in."

"How about Marta Howard?" I asked.

"Not in."

"When do you expect them?"

"Maybe later, maybe not."

"Where can I—"

Ronnie hung up before I could squeeze in the next question.

There was a pub fifty yards up from BeeJay's with outdoor tables. I dropped a five-pound note on the bar and, on the theory of "when in Rome", ordered a pint of bitter. The bartender, a burly guy in a plaid wool shirt, ran off a string of unintelligible brand names. I pointed at one of the half-dozen polished-brass draft handles, and he poured a brew the color of dark maple syrup, with a thick, foamy head.

I scooped up most of the coins he gave me for change, wondering if the tip I left was too much or too little, then carried the beer to one of the outside tables.

As a stakeout site, this was about as good as you could get. There was a statue of a man on a horse in the middle of the street, around which gathered a group of young men and women, teens to early twenties, with large, industrial-type electronic pagers holstered on their belts, leaning against their bicycles and motor-cycles: on-call messengers waiting for the next run. I sat down on one of the white-plastic molded chairs and watched the front of BeeJay's for a half an hour. Business was good. There was no sign of Gurbeep Singh, and though dozens of women who could have been Marta Howard entered the store, they all left within a very short period, most carrying shopping bags with "BeeJay's" stenciled in orange against a white background.

To my surprise, I found that heavy, room-temperature beer wasn't all that bad. I got a refill and resumed my surveillance, learning nothing other than that BeeJay's was a going concern. I drained the last of the beer and decided that I'd either have to go back to the yellow pages and hope to find someone a little more reliable than George Proctor, or go to work myself.

Lazy as the beer was making me, I decided to go to work. I went into a shop down the street, bought a cheap red vinyl jacket, and, being a loyal fan, from the multitude of American baseball hats picked one with a San Francisco Giants logo on it.

I bundled my sport coat into the store's bag, then went in search of my next purchase, having to travel almost three blocks before I found a florist. A dozen long-stemmed roses were priced at what should have paid for a good meal for two with wine, so I settled on red carnations, which went for a pound each. I filled out one of the flower-shop's cards in bold print, "For Marta, Love, Nick," stuck it amid the carnations, then addressed an envelope simply to "G. Singh" and headed back to Carnaby Street.

"Want to make a quick ten bucks?" I asked one of the messengers, who was astride his motorcycle chewing on a candy

25

bar. He had frizzy blond hair tied back in a ponytail so tight it made his eyes slant.

"Huh? Ten bucks?"

I remembered where I was. "Five pounds." I handed him the envelope with Singh's name on it and pointed to BeeJay's. "Just go down there and deliver this to a Mr. Singh."

He eyed me suspiciously, taking in the flowers under my arm. "You kidding me, mate?"

I held the five-pound note under his nose. "Nope. Just go in there. Ask for Mr. Singh in a loud voice. If he's not there, ask where he is, or when he'll be back."

He sucked in his lower lip and thought it over. I waved the note slowly back and forth to help him make his decision. He got off his motorcycle as if it were a horse that might start kicking at any time, and grabbed the money and envelope in one swish. "Why the fuck not?"

Why not, indeed? I followed right behind him as he entered BeeJay's. There were several customers. Ronnie was behind the counter punching merrily away at the cash register. The messenger lumbered up to him and moved his lips. What came out sounded reasonably like "Where's Mr. Singh? Got a message for him."

Ronnie gave him a look that might have withered timid customers but had no affect on my man. "Where's Singh?" he repeated loudly. "Not here," he said, smiling hopelessly at the young woman he was taking money from.

"When will he be back?" the messenger dutifully asked.

I jumped in, holding the flowers up in front of my face, and, in a voice I hoped sounded somewhat like the bike messenger's, said: "Delivery for Marta Howard. She said she wanted them in water right away. Got something I can put them in?"

Ronnie tilted his head back and whirled it in exasperation. "Really, can't you boys see I'm busy?" He pointed a red-nailed finger at the messenger. "Mr. Singh isn't in. Leave whatever you have." The finger moved in my direction. "You. There's a vase and a washstand in back. Take care of those, will you, please?"

I wouldn't have figured that "please" was a word in Ronnie's vocabulary. I walked around the counter, through a curtained doorway, and into a honeycomb of small rooms. A tattered brown-and-beige-tweed hall runner lay on the concrete floor. The first two rooms were filled with boxed merchandise.

The door to the next room was locked, securely locked, with a top of the line Kaba Gemini cylinder door lock and an additional deadbolt. It would be easier and faster to saw through the walls than try and pick those babies. The Gemini systems use special keys, not like the ones you use for your house and car, with those sharp little tumbler cuts. With the Kaba system the key blades are dimpled on the top and bottom edges, as well as both sides, with shallow little craters carved out of the metal in different sizes and depths that fit precisely into the lock's fifteen pins. To make it even harder, the lock's internal pins are made of hardened steel, making drilling them out a problem. I knocked on the door: metal, as was the door casing.

Luckily, the last room was unlocked, the door wide open. The were two black metal desks with four matching file cabinets against the wall. I dropped the flowers on top of the cabinets and began digging through the first desk. Lots of business-related papers, all showing the name BeeJay's. Nothing under Carlisle, Inc., and nothing showing the names Gurbeep Singh or Marta Howard.

I flipped through the Rolodex. No Carlisle, Inc., or Singh, but there was a card with the name Marta. No address, just a phone number. I plucked the card from the Rolodex and pocketed it. A business-appointment calendar was open to the pages for the current week. Under today's date was a scribbled notation, "Rules—8." The rest of the week was blank. I took a last look around the room and left. Ronnie gave me a scornful glance on the way out. It must have been the Giants cap.

"Rules, sir," said the Ritz Hotel's concierge, "considers itself London's oldest restaurant. It was one of Lily Langtry's favorites. A very good choice. May I make reservations for you?"

"Yes, tonight at eight." I passed a ten-pound note into his gray-gloved hands. He protested mildly.

27

"If you can arrange a seat for me next to a table reserved by either a Mr. Singh or a Ms. Howard, I'd appreciate it."

He nodded his elegantly barbered head. "Consider it done, sir."

I went back to my room and called the number on the Rolodex card for the fifth time. Same result: a recorded, no-nonsense, feminine voice saying: "Hi, I'm out. You know what to do." What to do was wait for the beep and leave a message. Since I had already left two messages, I just hung up.

I looked at the phone book again, debating whether to try finding another private detective to get an address for the phone number. Every investigator worth his weight in trench coats had a source at the phone company to get unlisteds, or nonpubs, as they're called in the trade. Illegal, of course, but one of the necessary tools of the trade. Were London private eyes more law-abiding? More aware of the right of individuals to privacy? Less greedy? No. Proctor had proved that. So, if nothing turned up at Rules, I'd have to go shopping again.

5.

Rules was located on a small, narrow street in the Covent Garden area. It didn't look all that impressive on the outside, but once in the door the feeling and smell of old money permeated the air. The greeter had the smile of a restaurateur who didn't have to worry about newspaper reviews or food trends. After you've been open for a hundred and eighty years or so, I guess you have to feel you're in business to stay. The burgundy walls were overlayed with Edwardian paintings, gilt-framed mirrors, and original cartoons that looked like they could have graced the pages of the *New Yorker*.

My reservation was confirmed, my raincoat was shuffled off to the cloakroom, and I was convoyed through several small, crowded rooms to a table at the back of the restaurant. There was that pleasant restaurant sound, a combination of hushed conversations, corks being popped, glasses clinking, forks scraping against heavy china. The table was set with snow white linen, the plates, silverware, and glasses set out in military precision.

The waiter hovered long enough to see that I was comfortably seated before taking my drink order. I glanced around at my neighbors. The table directly alongside was empty. The rest of the room was filled with very well dressed, middle-aged couples and groups of male diners, some looking like they could have posed for the cartoons on the walls.

I'd been warned against ordering martinis in London. "They'll come warm and half-filled with vermouth!" The waiter must have seen the "made in USA" union label on my coat, because the drink was dusty-dry and properly chilled.

The menu was long and varied, with a special section devoted to game, everything from quail, partridge, and pheasant to boar and deer, all coming from the restaurant's own game preserve. Somehow that brought forth an image of all those cute little animals lined up in queues waiting to hear from the kitchen what the specials were that night.

Of course, the Dover sole I was contemplating probably wasn't thrilled when he and his buddies were wrapped up in that net. Some scientists swore that with the proper electronic instruments you could hear a carrot make gut-wrenching sounds when it was pulled from the ground. So, as long as I was going to feel guilty no matter what I ate, I decided on the Aberdeen Angus beef.

I was giving my order to the waiter when a young woman with shortish ash-blond hair, the bangs swooping down almost to her eyebrows, sat down at the empty table next to mine. She was wearing a smartly tailored maroon silk dress with balloon sleeves. She surveyed the room while taking off her brown leather gloves, her pale-blue eyes flicking over me briefly before continuing her tour. One thing was for sure. If she was Marta Howard, she certainly didn't do her personal shopping at BeeJay's.

She glanced at her watch, tapping her long fingers against the tablecloth, a look of impatience settling in on her finely chiseled features. The waiter was ladling out my soup with all the delicacy of an altar boy pouring wine into a bishop's chalice. My blond neighbor ordered a glass of wine and began checking her watch every minute or so. She was not the type who liked to be kept waiting, not the type men stood up.

I gave her what I thought was my most charming smile. "Looks like both our dining companions are late. I hope they're not somewhere together." She gave me a drop-dead look, soft blue eyes turning the color of ice stuck to the roof of a freezer.

I kept the smile stitched onto my face. "I was supposed to meet Gordy Singh, but I guess he's going to be a no show."

Both eyebrows were raised, disappearing completely under her bangs. "Gordy? Gordy was going to meet you here?"

"Yes. My name's Polo, Nick Polo. You wouldn't happen to be Marta Howard, would you?"

The eyes narrowed and got cold again. "You left a message on my machine, didn't you?"

"Yes, I did." I waved a palm toward the empty seat at my table. "Would you care to join me while we wait for Gordy?"

She considered the request for a full minute before tightening her lips and giving me a half-smile. She stood up, holding her wineglass, leaned over my shoulder, and in a soft, sexy voice said, "Stay away from me, you son of a bitch," all the while slowly emptying her wineglass into my lap. The wine flowed in a steady stream, and all the time those blue orbs of hers were locked onto mine. "Just stay away." She put the empty glass down with a bang, swiveled her hips, and walked away at the same pace that Ricky Henderson runs out ground balls to the shortstop.

There are several things you can do at a time like that: Call her all the descriptive, four-letter words that immediately jump into your mind. Run after her and return the compliment with a wine bucket. Or do what I did: Sit there and pretend that nothing unusual has happened. Dear old Marta had been so nonchalant about the whole thing that no one in the restaurant had noticed her wine-in-the-pants trick. I dropped my napkin down below and tried to mop up the excess without looking too much like a sex pervert about to assault a game hen.

The waiter seemed to notice something was amiss. "Everything all right, sir?"

"Terrific. Would you bring the wine list, and another napkin?" I took as long as possible over dinner, sipping wine, wiping my lap, sipping soup, wiping my lap. Eat and wipe, all the way through the main course and a dessert of whisky-and-ginger ice cream. Then brandy and coffee, interspersed with a request for yet another napkin.

Luckily I'd worn the darkest of my two pairs of gray slacks. I walked quickly, holding a menu discreetly in front of me, and made it to my raincoat and safely out the door without anyone starting to tell pee-in-your-pants jokes. It was only after I was a half-block away from Rules that I let out a streak of those descriptive, four-letter words directed at Marta Howard.

I called Raymond Singh in San Francisco as soon as I came back to the world of the living. London time was 10:30 A.M., which meant it was 2:30 A.M. in San Francisco. Under the circumstances, I didn't mind interrupting Raymond's sleep. But the groggy young feminine voice that answered the phone had no idea where he was or when he would be back.

"Tell him Nick Polo called from London. I'm having trouble running down the party he wanted me to see. Tell him it may take a couple more days."

She repeated the message back to me, then hung up without a goodbye.

I was in no mood to face the iron maidens in the Palm Room that morning, so I ordered breakfast from room service. I was studying my reflection in the mirror, the razor blade scraping my Adam's apple, when the phone rang.

It was my money expert from Southern California. "Got a pencil?" he asked.

A pencil? At the Ritz? I picked up the elegantly engraved chrome pen and said, "Shoot."

"Carlisle, Inc. Interesting outfit. Your boy Gurbeep Singh is the main man. Here are the other individuals authorized to sign checks. I'll go slow and spell them out." Good thing he did, transmitting the names Deepak Yadav, Gurdawer Mand, Jasbir Bhatt, and my personal favorite, Jagdeep Sidhu. "One other guy," he added. "Oliver Trent. Singh and Trent handle most of the action."

"What about addresses?"

"Almost everything came out to an address on Carnaby Street." He gave me the number for BeeJay's. "The other address, and this was used only once a few months ago, is something called 25 the Holtons, Kensington. Not just plain old 25 Holtons. The Brits have to stick 'the' in there."

"Anything else interesting?" I asked.

"Your boy Gurbeep goes through a lot of money. Transfers it around a lot. Works on a Swiss account. Most of the action centers from London, but he gets a lot of action out of India. Wait a minute." I could hear the rustling of papers. "Yeah, Calcutta, Bombay, all over the place. Vancouver, your town, Frisco, and some dump in Northern California called Yuba City."

Yuba City? I vaguely knew it was a hundred or so miles northeast of San Francisco and was once famous for its fruit trees. What the hell did Yuba City have in common with cosmopolitan metropolises like London, Calcutta, Bombay, Vancouver, and San Francisco?

"What else am I getting for my money?"

"Don't get snotty, Polo. You're lucky you're getting this much. There's a yellow flag on old Gurbeep's account."

I knew a yellow flag was what a referee dropped in a football game when one or two of the boys were caught doing something naughty, but I had no idea what it meant on someone's bank records.

"The police have expressed an interest," he explained. "A big interest. So I had to get in and out real quick. I'll tell you one thing I saw before I exited the database. Singh cashes a lot of checks at a place called Blackwell's in London."

The Ritz concierge knew the name right away. "A gambling establishment, sir. On Archer Street."

"Private?"

"All the casinos in London are private, to some extent."

"Can you arrange to get me a temporary membership?"

He nodded his handsome head a few inches. "Certainly, sir." He rolled his right hand into a fist, brought it to his lips, and coughed gently. "There is a dress code," he said discreetly, eyes traveling a straight line from my shirt collar to shoes.

"Point well taken," I said, assessing the damage done to my

limited wardrobe in the last two days. My blue blazer was looking a little seedy, the gray slacks were a little too light for what London might consider proper evening attire, and the Rockport loafers were in terrible need of a shine. Would Raymond Singh consider a new wardrobe a legitimate expense? How many "no problems" can you expect out of one man?

6

.

I don't know whether it was the shortest route to 25 the Holtons, but it was certainly worth the ride. The cabby, a broad-shouldered young guy wearing khaki pants and a dark-blue T-shirt, was obviously more concerned with showing off his muscles than in keeping warm. He drove me alongside a surprisingly dry-grassed park and skirted around Buckingham Palace, past a massively impressive building he identified in a bored voice as the Victoria and Albert Museum. Next to that was a pleasant blending of old-world charm and ultra-modern design housing the Natural History Museum.

We continued on through an area filled with tall, well-kept houses, pulling up to the curb in front of a white, four-story brick-and-stucco affair bordered by an eight-foot fence of lacy black wrought iron. The cabby twisted around, giving me the once-over, much as the hotel's concierge had. "This the place you wanted?" he asked doubtfully.

"I hope so," I replied, giving him one of the heavy one-pound coins as a tip. Then I waited until he drove away before climbing the black-painted brick steps to the front door.

The paint on the brick was peeling, and pockets of dry rot

were leaking through the overhanging balcony. Lavender wisteria cascaded down the left side of the house, obscuring the windows. Two oversized, weather-pitted black metal outdoor lights bracketed the front door. Both fixtures were curtained with spider webs. Judging from the number of flies in the webs, the spiders were in for a good feed.

I couldn't find a doorbell, so I pounded away on the heavy oak door. After a few minutes it opened wide enough to show a short, bent-over woman in a dusty white sari. She bowed her head and said something I couldn't understand.

"Mr. Singh, please."

Her head bobbed sideways. A sad smile creased her leathery face. "No, no," she said in a voice barely above a whisper.

"Mr. Oliver Trent, then," I said, edging my foot into the doorway.

She stayed bent over, backing up slowly, her head in constant motion.

"Do you understand me?" I said slowly, moving into the house. "I want to see Mr. Gurbeep Singh or Oliver Trent. Will you please tell them I'm here?"

Fear showed in her large, dark eyes.

"Just tell them I'm here. There is no trouble," I said, smiling as sincerely as I could.

She shuffled backward toward a door at the end of the hall. The heads of two children, no more than seven years of age, both with pitch-black hair, peeked around the door frame. She whispered something to them and closed the door firmly.

I took a look around. Scuffed hardwood floors butted up against pale-gray walls in need of paint. A heavy crystal chandelier hovered above, more than half of its flame-shaped bulbs burned out.

The door that the old woman had gone through opened with a snap and a squat, powerfully built man in his mid-thirties marched into the room. He wore dark slacks and a white dress shirt buttoned to the neck. The top of his bald head glistened under the long strands of hair that were slicked across it. Either his nose was scarred from smallpox or some tiny animals had

36

been chewing on it. He kept coming until he was no more than a foot away.

"What is it you want?" he said in a thick accent that I assumed was Indian.

"Gurbeep Singh. I'm here to see Gurbeep Singh."

"What do you want?" he demanded, puffing his chest out like a canary about to reach for a high note.

"His cousin Raymond sent me. I have some money for him."

"How much money?"

"A lot."

He let out a long breath of air, his chest returning to its normal position. "I am Gurbeep Singh."

"I don't think so."

The chest puffed out again.

I reached inside my sport-coat pocket for the picture Raymond had given me, slowing down my fingers to crawling speed when I saw his hand dart toward his back pants pocket.

Raymond Singh had told me that Gurbeep had a circular scar around his left nipple, but the thought of seeing this guy bare-chested was not all that appealing. "I have a picture," I explained, taking the photograph out with two fingers and holding it toward him. "Raymond told me that the other man in the picture is Gurbeep Singh."

He studied the picture for several seconds, then said: "Raymond made a mistake. That is our cousin, Raman Singh."

I held out a hand for the picture, which he returned reluctantly. "Raymond doesn't make many mistakes. Do you have some identification?"

He shook his head, sending a few strands of hair falling across his ears. "You don't believe me?"

"How about Oliver Trent? Maybe he can help clear this matter up."

His straightened to his fullest height, then grumbled nastily, "How did you hear of Oliver Trent?"

"Raymond gave me the name."

"Get out!"

"Not until I see Gurbeep—"

His hand flashed to his back pocket and he pulled out one of those Philippine butterfly knifes, the type with a blade surrounded on both sides by a split handle. He flicked his wrist expertly and the six-inch blade was pointed at my belly button. "Out," he said, gesturing with the knife and shepherding me toward the door.

I did exactly what the self-defense expert at the police academy had told us to do in a situation like this. "Yes, sir," I said, backpedaling as fast as I could without tripping.

A look of contempt came over his face as he watched me awkwardly grope for the doorknob. "Do not come back," he threatened once I was safely outside the house.

"Gurbeep will want Raymond's money. What do you want me to do with it?" His suggestion was predictable and would have made for an uncomfortable walk back to the Ritz if I had followed it.

London is a walking town, relatively flat, with something well worth looking at on every corner. I feasted my eyes, stopping every few blocks to ask one of the cheery locals to point me in the right direction and let my brain run through the lists of should haves and would haves. I should have run a financial and criminal check on Gurbeep Singh before I left San Francisco. I should have run an up-to-date check on Raymond Singh, too. I should have asked around, found someone who was connected with the London police or Scotland Yard. I should have found someone who knew a reliable private investigator in London. I would have done all that, I reluctantly admitted, but I was just too lazy. Besides, Raymond Singh had pushed the right button, my greed button. I was reminded of one of my father's oft-repeated pieces of advice, "If it sounds too good to be true, you can bet your ass it is too good to be true."

When I got back to the hotel I tried calling Raymond Singh again in San Francisco. The same sweet voice I had spoken to last time told me Raymond was still out. She sounded a little worried this time. "Have him get in touch with me right away," I told her. "It's important."

I went over the list of names of people who were authorized

to write checks on the Carlisle, Inc., account: Deepak Yadav, Gurdawer Mand, Jasbir Bhatt, Jagdeep Sidhu, Oliver Trent. What a group. I checked each name in the phone book. None were listed.

Back home I'd have had my fingers flying across my computer keyboard, running each name through a series of data checks. With names like those, something should pop up. Especially those unusual first names.

You want to pull a disappearing act? Get a common name, very common: Smith, Jones, Lee. But make sure that the first name is just as common—Mary, James, Joseph—because a lot of the data sources are keyed to that first name. Throw in a first initial and you're even harder to find, like, say, "T. James Smith." Computer databases balk at that first initial. It gives them too many choices, everything from Tammy to Teresa to Tuesday to Thomas to Thelonious to Theodore and on and on.

I considered my options: a solo stakeout on 25 the Holtons, or somehow getting an address for Marta Howard. Which meant looking for another local private investigator. I went shopping in person this time and found my man on my third stop. His office was a combination office-apartment on the third floor of a rather shabby building on Clerkenwell Road. The building's tenants were a varied mix: a beauty shop, a literary agency, a realtor, sales representatives, and one private detective, William Fields.

The other tenants had their names painted in either gold leaf or black letters on their glass-front doors. Fields simply had a business card Scotch-taped to his unvarnished door. The office itself was cluttered with a combination of metal filing cabinets and overstuffed couches draped with discarded slacks and sweaters. An old Dick Haymes song, "It Might as Well Be Spring," was spinning away on an expensive-looking stereo system.

"Can I help you?" a weatherworn-looking man in his early fifties asked me. He had a tousled mess of gray hair and wore a tan cardigan over a yellow turtleneck. He had the look of a man who'd been around, knew the ropes, and didn't mind taking chances, the look of a man who, if not in his chosen line of work, might sell items that fell off the backs of trucks.

"Mr. Fields?"

"Right. Sorry for the mess. Don't get many callers in this trade."

How right he was. Most private investigators subsist on a steady diet of attorneys and insurance adjusters. The attorneys are too busy to go to your place and the insurance people want you over at their offices to review the files to be worked on and then to take them to lunch, so you can properly thank them for the assignment.

I handed Fields my card. He studied it briefly, not looking overly impressed. "Bit out of your bailiwick, ain't you?"

"Way out. That's why I need your help." It took me only a few minutes to explain to Fields what I wanted. I laid out five twenty-pound notes, and another of my cards, with Marta Howard's telephone number written on the back, on the arm of his sofa.

"Getting that kind of information would be illegal, Mr. Polo," he said with a knowing grin.

"Not necessarily," I said, giving him a scenario that would get him off the hook. "Going through the phone company to get an unlisted number would be. But if you somehow asked around, found someone who knew Marta Howard, and that someone gave you the address to go with that phone number, there certainly wouldn't be anything illegal in that."

Fields found a stray piece of thread on his cardigan's sleeve, plucked it off, and dropped it, watching it spiral to the carpet.

"If you can get me the number within half an hour, there's another twenty pounds in it for you."

His watery blue eyes stared lovingly at the small stack of money. Dick Haymes was into "The Very Thought of You."

"That the *Rain or Shine* album?" I asked Fields.

His eyes bounced up to mine. "You like Haymes?"

"Just a notch below Sinatra when it came to ballads."

Fields had found a soul brother. He regaled me for five minutes on why the great American pop singers of the past were still big in England, while Americans ignored them.

"The telephone number, Mr. Fields. I need that address."

"There's a pub round the corner. Meet you there in twenty minutes."

40

Fields's source at the London phone company was fast. He was there in under ten minutes, calling out to the bartender: "Large whiskey, Johnny, and give this gentleman whatever he wants. My treat."

He handed me one of his business cards. "The address is on the back," he said. Then he added: "What about Bobby Darin? You like him? I saw him once. Did a show here in London. Another Yank who died too young. Everybody's either dead or getting old. Bloody shame, ain't it?"

"Bloody right," I agreed.

I spent some plastic money at one of the posh shops off the Ritz's lobby: new navy-blue blazer, slacks, shirts, and a black raincoat, all at prices that would have made me wince if they had been in dollars. I winced double since they were in pounds, then set out for the address William Fields had developed from Marta Howard's phone number.

The apartment house was of granite blocks, six stories high. The name Marta Howard was inscribed on a polished brass marker next to apartment 3C. There was a liquor store down the street. I bought a bottle of Moët et Chandon champagne and went back to Marta Howard's apartment.

The front door was locked, naturally, and I was wondering whether I should try and slip the lock or just buzz her and see if she'd let me in, when a happy-looking young couple dressed for an evening on the town exited, the young man showing respect for his elders by holding the door open for me as I hustled inside. A small metal bird-cage elevator grunted and clanged me up to the third floor. I tapped lightly on Marta Howard's door. After a minute a voice inquired, "Who is it?"

The trick in getting someone to open their door is not to give them a long answer, so they can't identify the voice as one they don't know. Also, you have to give them an answer they can believe, one that one of their friends or loved ones might use. "Me," I said in a grunt.

The door swung open. Whoever Marta Howard had dressed for, he was a lucky man. Cherry-red silk, scooped at the neck. Matching gloves climbing up to her elbows. A diamond necklace wrapped around her neck, with matching tear-shaped earrings. Her face was frozen in a half-smile.

"Hi, Marta," I said, holding the bottle of champagne toward her as a peace offering. "I don't know what happened at the restaurant, but I'd really like to talk to you about—"

She screamed those three magical words "Help! Rape! Police!" Then she slammed the door, smashing the champagne bottle and sending shards of glass and a shower of wine all over the walls, the carpet, and my new raincoat. I was pounding down the stairs as the first of the neighboring doors popped open.

7
.

I was becoming addicted to those charming London taxi-cabs. The driver, a likable old duffer named Mike, chewed my ear off for nearly an hour, giving me a crash course in soccer, local politics, the sex lives of the royal family, the names of the best restaurants and the best whorehouses, and an update on the climate.

"Don't really get the fog much anymore," Mike said. "Making a bloody motion picture in Soho the other day, one of those thrillers, you know, dark alleys, murky shadows, one of those ripper things. Had to bring in a bloody fog machine." He swiveled around to make sure I got the point. "A fog machine. Can you believe it?"

"Strange," I agreed.

He settled back in front of his steering wheel. "Most folks blame it on that world-heatin'-up stuff. But it's the coal, mate. We just don't burn as much as we used to. Cleaning up the town, we is."

Mike turned the conversation to American football. "Big, tough-looking buggers," he said, "but they should be, all bundled up with those corsets and pads. Helmets like the bloody

43

knights used to wear in combat. Soccer, now, that's different. Nothing to protect you in soccer. None of those damn padded costumes."

We were sitting a half-block down from the entrance to Marta Howard's apartment house. In the few moments when Mike wasn't talking, the loudest sound to be heard was passing traffic and the clicking of the cab's meter. Marta hadn't been dressed for an evening at home by the fire. Of course, my appearance might have canceled her plans, but at the moment staking her out seemed to be my best bet.

Mike was back into sexual politics, midway into a story about a transvestite member of Parliament, when a huge black limousine pulled up in front of Marta Howard's place. The man from 25 the Holtons, the one with the Philippine butterfly knife, got out of the driver's door, slammed it shut, peered up and down both sides of the street, then disappeared inside the building.

"What kind of car is that, Mike?"

"Daimler. Makes a Rolls look grotty, don't it?"

I'd heard of Daimlers, no doubt seen them in movies, but this was my first in-person look. Impressive, with a sloping trunk that Cadillac had tried copying back in the seventies.

"You know the driver?" Mike asked.

"I met him once."

"Must have lots of the green stuff. King's ransom, those lovelies cost."

"If the driver comes out of the apartment house with a blond woman, we'll be following them, Mike."

He revved up his engine. "No problem keepin' in sight of that beauty."

Marta and the Daimler's driver came out a few minutes later. He held the back door open for her before getting behind the wheel. Traffic was at its usual hectic pace, but Mike did a professional job of keeping them in sight. If the Daimler's driver was looking for a tail, he'd have a tough time distinguishing Mike's cab from the dozens of clones racing up and down the dark London streets.

"Where are we?" I asked Mike.

44

"The Strand. He's turning right toward Covent Garden. Lots of theaters round here. Probably taking the lady to a show."

We moved slowly through narrow streets, the sidewalks overflowing with pedestrians. "Looks like the Royal Opera for them," Mike said, slowing down as the Daimler pulled to a stop.

The driver got out and opened the door for Marta Howard, who stood and looked around as if she were expecting to meet someone. I passed two twenty-pound notes to Mike. "That cover it?"

"More than, mate. Thanks."

I mingled within the crowd, watching as the big limousine purred away. Howard kept twisting her neck as she walked slowly up to the lobby of the Royal Opera. There was an excited buzz in the air, and people struggled out of coats and patted pockets for tickets as they approached the lobby.

Marta Howard waved a gloved hand in greeting and was shortly in the arms of a dark-haired man, about her height, dressed in a black raincoat. As they hugged he turned my way and before he nuzzled her neck. I got a view of his face: Gurbeep Singh himself. They locked arms and went into the theater. I tried following, only to be stopped by a uniformed usher who said, "Ticket, please, sir."

"I'm not seeing the show. Just wanted to say something to a friend who just went in."

He smiled with his mouth but not his eyes. He had heard that one, along with a lot better ones, many times before.

"Sorry, sir. No admittance without a ticket."

"Where can I buy a ticket?"

His eyes opened up on that one. "For tonight's performance, sir? You must be joking. Sold out for months." He waved me away with a hand. "Don't block the aisle, please, sir."

They say, and I had always believed them, that there is not an event in the world you can't get into, if you're willing to pay the price. Just show up, whether for the seventh game of the World Series, a Superbowl game, a heavyweight championship match, or a hot Broadway play of the moment. Wave enough cash and you're in.

I had always believed this until that moment, trying to get

a ticket to the Royal Opera. Some people looked as if they were going to call a bobby when I popped the question to them. Others just gave me an amused smile and a shake of the head. Where were the scalpers? What was the matter with British entrepreneurship? Hadn't they learned anything from Thatcher?

I went back and pestered another usher, who told me that the performance ran a little over three hours, with an intermission roughly halfway through. Three hours. I checked my watch. That would make it eleven, if Gurbeep and Howard were true opera fans and didn't duck out early. I circled the block, looking for the black Daimler. Not around. Either the driver knew just when to come back and pick them up or his duties were over for the night.

I could not hear any music coming from the Royal Opera itself, but there was the distinct blaring of an aria coming from down the street. I followed my ears to a big, open square. A portable power unit was projecting a scene against a brick wall, showcasing a large, heavily wigged gentleman and an equally large, heavily wigged lady, lambasting each other with rich, powerful voices. A good-sized crowd was standing by watching, some holding glasses of beer or wine in their hands, others drinking right from the bottle.

I wandered a little further. A ring of spectators had formed a circle around a bare-chested elderly man in dark work pants. There were thick, heavy chains wrapped around his chest and arms. A younger man with a strong resemblance to the old-timer was snapping shut oversized padlocks on the chains. The old-timer kept a line of patter going, drawing loud roars from the crowd. I couldn't understand one word he said, but everyone appeared to be having a great time.

It took him some ten minutes to get trussed up, his young helper stopping his chores long enough to make repeated trips into the audience with hat in hand. I dropped a couple of pound coins into the fast-filling chapeau. The old-timer grunted and groaned and arched his back in pain, fell to the cobbled street, rolled around, and finally jumped to his feet, free of his chains, drawing hearty cheers and more coin of the realm.

Before he was through picking up his props, two young

jugglers, dressed as if they'd just left Robin Hood's hideout in Sherwood Forest, jumped into the circle and started their act.

It was as pleasant a way as any to kill time while I waited for the opera to end. I watched a few more street artists: acrobats, singers, banjo players. Then I wandered around Covent Garden's stores, a combination of smart shops and flea markets, making two purchases: a plaid hat worthy of Henry Higgins's head and a cheap pipe.

I had some pub grub, steak and kidney pie at a nice little place called Porter's, and was back at the entrance to the Royal Opera at a quarter after ten, my disguise kit firmly in place. A hat is always good. You can tilt it and cover half of your face. The pipe is a good idea too, because it draws people's attention to it, and not your facial features. So I paced around, sucking on the pipe's dry stem. There was no sign of the Daimler. As soon as the opera ended and the crowd erupted from the building, I knew I was in trouble. They scattered in all directions, like birds flushed by a hunter's dog. I was pushed and shoved back and forth as I tried holding my ground, finally catching a glimpse of what looked like Marta Howard's blond coiffure bobbing among the throng. I kept shoving and then standing on my toes trying to keep her in sight, losing her completely as, within minutes, the vast number of people vanished, disappearing into cars, restaurants, pubs, and unknown doorways. Where the hell had they gone? I circled the block twice. No sign of Singh, Marta, or the Daimler.

Think, Polo, I advised myself calmly. Where would you go with a beautiful woman after an evening at the opera? Back to her place, I hope, I answered truthfully. Cheapo. How about expending a little money and charm on the lady? Dinner. Dancing. Something fun. Maybe a little gambling.

Saved by another London cabby. "Do you know where Blackwell's casino is?" I asked the not too friendly gentleman.

"I do," he answered with little enthusiasm.

I hopped into the back of his cab. "Let's go, then."

He gave me a smile showing a gap of missing teeth on the top, turned on his meter, then turned it off almost immediately after traveling all of ten feet.

"Shortest trip I ever made," he said, pointing a stubby index finger out of his window. "There's Blackwell's, mate. Across the street."

The name "Blackwell's" was barely visible, discreet white lettering on a gray placard hanging over the entrance of a brick building. The man behind the desk in the foyer was wearing a well-cut pearl-gray tuxedo. He appeared to be the proper gentleman except for a nose that looked as if it had been busted several times and reset by a carpenter.

"Nick Polo," I told him. "The Ritz Hotel advised me I might have a good time here."

He played around with a computer, saw my name on the screen, and smiled. "Membership fees are fifty pounds, Mr. Polo."

I counted out the necessary pieces of paper, noting that it was time to start cashing in some travelers' checks. He took my hat and champagne-spotted raincoat without a word, and I was directed "through those doors and upstairs."

While neither the outer shell of the building nor the little lobby of Blackwell's was very impressive, once through those doors you were transported into a different world. The entrance hall was huge, the floor a glossy gray terrazzo. A square, glass-topped table, the base made of what looked like a stack of black bowling balls, stood in front of an eight-foot-wide stairway leading upstairs. I dropped to one knee, as if to tie a shoe, for a better look and saw a label, Brunswick. Damned if they weren't real bowling balls. The staircase had chrome handrails held up and spaced apart by more bowling balls.

Another pearl-gray tuxedo was waiting for me at the top of the stairs, looking every bit as fit for action as his counterpart in the foyer. "First-time visitor, Mr. Polo?"

"Yes."

"We offer American roulette, blackjack, and punto banco, sir. The cashier is over there."

The cashier accepted by travelers' checks and gave me three hundred pounds' worth of chips, all in twenty-pound denominations. "The minimum wager," I was informed.

Lovely young women wearing black-and-white French

maids' uniforms were tottering around in spike heels, somehow balancing sterling-silver trays and serving drinks. I helped myself to a glass of champagne and surveyed the gambling room.

The walls were of a gray to match the tuxedoed help. The ceiling was of smoked mirrors. There were three roulette tables, American-style, which simply means that the wheel has both a single zero and a double zero. European-style roulette is played with thirty-six numbers, one to thirty-six, and the wheel has a single zero. That extra American-style double zero may not sound like much, but since every time the little ivory ball lands in double zero the house automatically wins, the extra zero increases the casino's already hefty odds advantange. It's really a sucker's game, but glamorous, easy to play, and fun.

All three roulette tables were crowded with an elegantly dressed crowd of men and women. I made my one and only automatic sucker bet, dropping a chip onto the twenty-two black spot on the table's green baize layout: twenty-two black, the very number that Rick Blaine (played by Humphrey Bogart) had fixed on the wheel in his Café Américain so he could signal the croupier, Émile (Marcel Dalio), through a haze of cigarette smoke to let the young Romanian couple (Joy Page and Helmut Dantine) win enough money to pay the lecherous Captain Louis Renault (Claude Rains) for that all-important visa out of Casablanca, thus keeping the lovely bride out of Renault's clutches.

Nostalgia has its moments, but not where gambling is concerned. Twelve red was the winner, and the croupier raked in my chip along with dozens of other losers. I wandered around, finally catching sight of both Marta Howard and Gurbeep Singh at one of the six punto-banco tables.

Punto banco is just another name for chemin de fer and baccarat, a game that gives off delicious vibes of high-stakes hands won by young James Bond types using their skill and luck to break the banks of arch-villains. The very elegance of the game scares off a lot of gamblers, which is too bad, because it's really pretty simple. Sometimes called "blackjack for idiots," it's easy to play, and it gives the gambler the best odds against the house of any of the casino games.

The gambling table is kidney-shaped, covered with a rich

green baize, the edges padded with thick leather. Eight decks of cards, half red-backed, the other half blue-backed, are shuffled and placed in a mahogany box called a *sabot* (French for "shoe"). With eight decks of cards there is absolutely no way to count cards. Thus luck has a lot more to do with baccarat then with other forms of gambling.

There are three casino employees running the game, two of whom position themselves in the middle of the table and handle the chips, pay off the winners, and keep track of the commissions each player owes the house. The third is known as the caller, and he does just that, announcing the different hands and directing the use of the *sabot*.

There can be as many as twelve players, but only two hands are dealt, one to the man in temporary charge of the *sabot*, the other to the house, or bank. A player can bet on either set of cards, the bank's hand or player's hand. It was more fun in James Bond's day. Then the person holding the shoe was actually the "banker," and he was betting against all the rest of the players. But the casinos found that there was a lot of time lost in waiting for a Daddy Warbucks with enough money to operate as the bank, so they took the job over themselves and raked off a percentage of the winnings on each pot.

Basically, four cards are dealt out of the *sabot*, face down, two to the player, the other two to the bank. The player then turns his cards face up. The object of the game is simply to get your cards to total nine, which is as high as you can go, since tens and picture cards count as zero. So if you had, say, a five and a king, since the king counts as zero your total would actually be five.

In European-style baccarat, the player had a choice after looking at his cards. He could draw a third card or stay with what he had, do a little bluffing. Unfortunately, the American version has taken some of the fun out of it, virtually eliminating any strategy on the part of the player.

Anytime the player has a combination that adds up to one-two-three-four-five or zero, he has to draw a card. With a total of six or seven, the player has to stand. An eight or nine is called a natural, an automatic winner. The bank can't draw a card against eight or nine, and the player and those who bet with him are paid off in a straight one-on-one bet: bet a buck, win a buck. The bank has some similar automatic rules for drawing a card.

There was an opening across from Gurbeep Singh and Marta Howard. As soon as she saw me her, eyes turned glacial and she started whispering words of wisdom into Singh's ear. He barely flicked a glance at me, keeping his attention on the action at the table. I settled into a soft, wine-red velvet chair next to an angry-looking young man with a nose like a plowshare and started throwing out chips. A half-hour later I was some two hundred and thirty pounds ahead. Had I been betting in the same quantity as Singh, I would have been many thousands of pounds ahead. He chucked out piles of chips and lost almost every time.

He looked exactly like the man in the picture Raymond Singh had given me: a helmet of shoe-polish-black hair sprayed into place, bushy eyebrows that went up and down like Venetian blinds when he won a hand, a thin sliver of mustache under a pendulous nose. His tuxedo was tailor-made, a fact that he advertised by having the last button on each coat sleeve unbuttoned and rolled back slightly just to prove that they were real, working buttonholes, and so it was impossible to miss the heavy gold cufflinks when he reached for his chips. Somewhere back in history there must have been a reason for putting buttons on men's coat sleeves. Now they are about as useful as intelligent questions at a presidential press conference.

Marta Howard kept eyeballing bullets into my heart and humming into Gurbeep's ear. By the time he stood up from the table, I figured he had lost at least two thousand pounds. He sprinkled a few chips into the croupier's hand, then looked my way, waggling an index finger and mouthing the words "Let's talk."

8

■

Gurbeep Singh stood calmly, an easy smile coming to his face, rocking back and forth on his heels like a fighter waiting for the bell to ring. He looked exactly like the man in the picture. There was no need to have him expose his scar-circled nipple.

Marta Howard was beside him, erect, chin up, shoulders back, both hands clamped firmly on a red leather purse. She murmured a final warning in his ear, then sauntered away, back toward the gaming tables.

Gurbeep Singh said, "I understand you are interested in talking to me, Mr.—"

"Nick Polo. Your cousin Raymond Singh asked me to look you up." I patted my pocket. "I have something for you from Raymond."

"My, my. Raymond certainly put you through a lot of trouble, Mr. Polo." He craned his neck and fluttered a hand, like a bird taking flight, toward a small bar at the back of the room. "Let's have a drink and see what you have for me." Gurbeep Singh had a clipped, upper-class English accent, sounding as if he'd been instructed in the language by Alistair Cooke.

We settled into a pair of fiberglass tulip-shaped pedestal

chairs, and one of the long-legged cocktail waitresses came over to serve us. "Champagne all right with you?" Singh asked.

"Sure."

He gave the girl our order, and when she questioned him as to his brand preference he did the flutter thing with his hands. "The best, my dear. Just bring us the best."

Singh turned his attention back to me. "You are an enterprising young man, sir. How did you know I'd be here at Blackwell's?"

"Pure luck," I lied. "I was just out for a night on the town. The concierge at the Ritz suggested Blackwell's."

His head bobbed up and down like a robin going after a worm. "Really? What an extraordinary coincidence. And how did you find Marta's place. More luck?"

"No, that was hard work. She doesn't seem to like me, for some reason."

Singh chuckled dryly. "She mistook you for someone else, Mr. Polo. There are certain people I try to avoid. Had I known you were from Raymond, there would have been no problem."

"No problem." It was probably inscribed on the Singh family crest. "I'm curious," he continued, "as to how you got the address of the house in Kensington."

"25 the Holtons? More hard work."

The waitress came over with a bottle of Krug Grand Cuvée. Singh dropped a casino chip on her tray. "Put it on my bill, darling," he said, toasting her with his glass.

I took the envelope Raymond Singh had given me and slid it across the table. "There's a letter, a cassette tape, and a cashier's check in there. Raymond said you'd be interested in what's on the cassette. You already know the amount of the check."

"Do I?"

"I left a copy of it for you at BeeJay's."

Singh gave his padded shoulders an elegant shrug. "Yes, that was good of you. So Raymond thinks I'll be interested in what is on the cassette. Raymond is seldom wrong. How is he? Still acting like a poor shopkeeper?"

"He seems to keep busy." I passed him the player-recorder that Raymond Singh had provided me with.

Gurbeep Singh picked the little machine up in his fingers, examining it closely as if it were a rare artifact. "Have you listened to the tape, Mr. Polo?" he asked, his eyes boring into mine.

"Raymond played a few seconds of it. It's in Hindi. I couldn't understand a word."

He took a deep sip of his champagne, leaned forward, and said: "I must apologize on Miss Howard's behalf. She thought she was protecting me. Apparently she did you some damage." He waved a hand in the air, a circus master introducing the next act. "Come, Marta. Keep Mr. Polo company while I listen to what Raymond has to say."

The girl popped into sight. Gurbeep Singh turned his back to me and murmured something to her. She listened with her eyes almost closed. "Tell him you are sorry, my dear," Singh said. "He is a friend." He gave me a curt bow, then turned on his heel toward the casino.

Marta Howard's breath went out in a long sigh. "You must think I'm a complete idiot."

I watched a little nervously as she picked up Singh's champagne. "You are dangerous with a wineglass in your hand."

She gave me both dimples and a flash of white teeth. "Really, if I had known who you were. I'll have to make it up to you somehow. Mr. Polo. That sounds so formal. May I call you Nick?"

"Certainly."

She kept the dimples in place, sat up, and shuffled her chair around until it was right alongside mine. "How on earth did you ever find us here tonight?"

I repeated my story. "Pure luck. I felt like gambling. My hotel suggested this place. I was quite surprised to see you."

She raised her glass slowly toward me. "This is too good to spill," she said. "To a new friendship. Gordy says you're a friend of his cousin in the States."

"Right."

She topped off our glasses and kept working the pump, asking how I liked London, how I liked the Ritz, how I had found her address.

55

"You really startled me when you came to my door," she said, inching forward in her chair, her knees bumping mine.

"You looked like you were prepared for any emergency," I said.

Gurbeep Singh rejoined us, signaling for another glass. "Was the tape interesting?" I asked him.

Singh curled his tongue against his teeth and whistled softly. "Quite. A business transaction," he said, looking at Marta Howard. "Raymond is always very cautious about these things. Tell Raymond that his request will be handled as he wishes, but tell him never to—" He pursed his mouth for a moment, then pulled his lower lip in, between his teeth.

"Never what?" I prompted.

He dusted the arms of his tuxedo jacket. "Never mind. Just tell him it will be done." He looked at Marta Howard for a long moment, then turned his attention back to me. "Are you a gambler, Polo?"

"Yes, but I've had a pretty good run at the baccarat table. I think I'll call it a night."

Singh rubbed his hands together briskly, as if holding them over a warm fire. "I feel very lucky. Marta does not enjoy gambling. Perhaps you could do me a favor and escort her home. You do know her address," he added pointedly.

Marta Howard was in no hurry to go home. She gave the cabby instructions, then told me we were going to "a hot new club," which turned out to be in the basement of a large, raw concrete box of a building. The surrounding buildings, all of them old and made of soot-stained brick, looked as if they would collapse in a stiff wind.

"They're tearing down all the old places," Marta said, slipping the driver some money, "and replacing them with shit like this. Awful, isn't it?" I didn't have time to agree with her as she bolted down a half-dozen cement steps and through a wide, industrial-sized metal door. I followed her inside, grateful for the warmth but not for the acoustics.

Whoever ran the place had saved a fortune on decorating. The walls and floors were a match for the exterior: unfinished concrete. The ceiling was open, the heating ducts wrapped in

56

aluminum foil. Track lighting in reds, blues, and yellows blinked on and off at staggered intervals. Speakers were placed every few feet and blared out a heavy rock beat.

The clientele ran the gamut from teens to late seventies, the dress from Savile Row and Christian Dior to leather and homeless chic: tattered woolen coats, navy watch caps, and long woolen scarves. My favorite early sighting was a young woman with platinum hair done in cornrows and a bumblebee-striped black-and-yellow scarf around her neck. That was it, unless you counted her goose bumps, an activity that looked as if it appealed to an elderly gentleman in white tie and tails who was doggedly following her. He carried an umbrella, rolled up to pencil thinness, that he tapped against her buttocks every time the girl paused to talk to someone.

Marta weaved her way through the crowd, shaking a hand here, pecking a check there, patting a fanny every time she came across one that was exposed to the elements, which was fairly often. The rule that applies to nude beaches, that the people who go there should never be seen nude, didn't come into play here. The bare butts, be they male or female, were young, firm, and fully packed.

Marta introduced me as "my good friend Nicky" to whomever she thought might be interested. Not too many of them were. Somewhere along the way, my sporty tweed hat got knocked off. I last saw it rolling between the beefy, unshaven legs of a bearded man wearing a miniskirt and spike heels.

We finally made our way to the bar: plain, warped knotty-pine planks propped up on sawhorses. The bartenders were all refugees from Muscle Beach, in cutoff jeans, their bare upper bodies glistening under coats of baby oil.

Cases of liquor were stacked haphazardly against a wall. Champagne bottles floated in iced metal buckets. The glasses were tin cups, the kind that Jimmy Cagney used to scrape along the bars while yelling at the screws, waiting for that last meal before they led him to the electric chair.

"What do you think of it, Nick?" Marta asked, shrugging out of her fur coat.

"Different. Just open up?"

"Oh, yes. And it won't be here long. In a week or so we'll have to move." She dipped a finger into her tin cup, then ran it down her throat. Drops of champagne started a slow journey down her neck, coursing into her diamond necklace.

"Warm, isn't it?" she asked.

"Getting warmer all the time," I agreed, taking off my raincoat and dropping it over my shoulder. "Why don't—" My words were drowned out by the crowd going wild: shouts, cheers, boots pounding on the floor. Even the bartenders got into the act, slamming their fists into their chests the way Tarzan did before yodeling to Jane that he'd be home for supper.

I tried to see what the commotion was about. At the far end of the room a luminous stage curtain was slowly drawn open and a bamboo cage swung into sight. The crowd went crazy again. I turned to ask Marta what it was all about and found her staring toward the stage with glazed eyes.

The bamboo cage was hooked onto casters on the ceiling. Two muscle-bound guys oiled up like the bartenders pushed the cage toward the middle of the room. As it got closer I could see there was someone inside the damn cage, a dark-haired girl, her hands tied over her head and hooked to the top of the cage. She was wearing one of those *bustier* things that Madonna had turned into a fashion statement.

Marta tugged at my sleeve. "What do you think she'll go for?"

"Go for?"

She dipped her finger into her cup again, this time rubbing it into the very visible crease between her breasts. "It's an auction, darling. Didn't you know? A slave auction." She rubbed her finger, the one she'd dipped into her wine, across my lips. "Don't bother bidding, unless you feel kinky and want extra company." Marta looked at the girl in the cage. "Beautiful, isn't she?"

She was indeed. Naturally dark skin, the color of tea, glistened against the white bustier. Her hair was tied up in twin ponytails. Her eyes were big, vacant brown pools, staring straight ahead, seemingly seeing nothing, her lips open slightly like a fish's when treading water.

One of the oiled musclemen started shouting orders though a portable microphone. "All right, ladies and gentleman, all right. What have we got tonight? Bidding starts at fifty pounds."

There were shouts and screams, people waving hands in the air. Muscleboy kept nodding and yelling encouragement as the bids went up and up.

Marta grabbed my arm, her fingers kneading my biceps. "Not going to join in?"

"What if the girl in the cage doesn't want to be part of this? What if she doesn't like whoever it is that ends up buying her?"

Her fingers worked harder on my arm. "Oh, she'll like it, whoever it is. Believe me, she'll love it, really love it."

I looked at the girl again, kneeling, arms over her head, a blank look on her face. Those big eyes roaming slowly over the crowd, her tongue slipping snakelike out between her lips. She could have been anywhere from her mid-teens to her early twenties.

"I have a hundred and eighty-five pounds," shouted the man with the microphone.

I leaned down and asked Marta, "What does the high bidder do with her?"

"Why, anything he or she wants, of course. That's the point of the game, Nicky."

"A hundred and eighty-five pounds. Is that the last bid? Come on, people. Look at her. All yours for a measly hundred and eighty-five pounds. Surely there's someone who can—"

"Two hundred pounds," I shouted, surprised that my voice sounded so shaky.

"Two hundred pounds. Now, that's more like it," the auctioneer said, sticking his microphone into the cage and putting it to the girl's mouth. Her tongue flicked out and licked it.

"Oh, she's going to be worth every penny, Nicky," Marta said, her fingers traveling from my arm up to my neck.

9

.

Even up close and personal, you couldn't tell how old she was. The complexion and body tone said early teens. The dull eyes and worry lines on her forehead said much older.

"What's your name?" I asked her.

"Jasmine," she answered in a soft, compliant voice.

"She's a beauty, isn't she, Nicky?" Marta exclaimed, grabbing Jasmine's two ponytails and pulling her head back. "A real jewel. You did well to get her so cheap."

"Speaking of cheap, buddy," the muscled auctioneer chimed in. "Pay-up time."

I gave him his money, peeling off the bills from my gambling winnings at Blackwell's. He counted it out carefully, leered up at me, and said, "Have fun." His eyes took in Marta. "Seeing you're with Miss Howard, you know where to bring her in the morning."

We were standing in a cell-like room that was in back of the curtained stage. Furnishings were at a minimum: a chipped, white enamel bed frame, topped by a dirty blue-and-gray-striped mattress partially covered by a thin yellow blanket that was spotted with dark, ameba-shaped stains. Lengths of twisted black leather straps were tied to the ends of the bed frame. There was one small nightstand, holding a shadeless desk lamp and three ashtrays. The ashtrays were filled with cigarette butts. Not too many of the butts had filters. The top of the nightstand was scarred from top to bottom with thin, jagged razor-blade scratches. Three battered wooden straight-back chairs encircled the bed. The place stank of used dope and locker room body odors.

My mind was brought out of its wanderings by the popping of a flashbulb. The auctioneer grinned at me. "Just the one picture. Want to make sure you bring her back in the same shape you took her." He waved a jaunty hand. "Have fun, children."

When he opened the door I could hear the crowd roaring again. "Another auction?" I asked Marta.

"Yes," she murmured, going back to Jasmine, her hands caressing her face, traveling down her neck to her shoulders, then gently lowering the top of the *bustier*. "Show the nice gentleman your jewelry, Jasmine," she crooned.

The girl's breasts were small, the same tea color as her face and shoulders. The nipples on both breasts had been pierced with thin gold rings.

I slapped Marta's hands away and grabbed Jasmine by the chin, staring into those vacant, dead eyes.

"Where do you live, Jasmine?"

She looked bewildered.

"Where do you live?" I repeated, my voice a harsh croak. "Live? Here."

"What's the matter with you?" Marta demanded. Her face was flushed, and she was breathing deeply. "Are you crazy?"

"Yeah. Maybe. Do you know where she lives?"

Marta walked casually to the bed, plopping down on the mattress, pulling her long legs up under her. "Anywhere she can. Anywhere she's told to go. She'll do anything for you, Nicky. Anything. For us. You own her until tomorrow. She likes it this way. Don't you understand?"

I wiped my sweating palms on the sides of my jacket. "Yeah. I do. I just don't play your kinds of games, lady. I want to take this kid home. Jesus Christ, she's no more than sixteen."

62

Marta just stretched out on the bed, slowly grinding her buttocks into the mattress. "She's old beyond her years, Nicky. Believe me. She wants to please you. You like to please people, don't you, Jasmine?"

As if on cue, the girl came up to me, bowing her head in obedience. "I am here to please you, master."

"This place just doesn't make it," I said to Marta. "No telling what kinds of germs are nesting in that bed." That thought apparently hadn't entered her mind before. She bounced to her feet, dusting down her red silk dress with both hands.

"Let's get out of here," I said. "But we can't cruise around town with Jasmine dressed like this." I wrapped my raincoat around the girl's thin shoulders.

Marta said: "Wait right here. I'll get my coat."

Once she was out of the room I went back to the Jasmine. "Do you have any friends, anyone who can take care of you?"

"You will take care of me," she said softly.

I grabbed her hand, turning the palm up, looking for needle marks on her arm. There were none, just smooth skin. Maybe they were shooting her up between her toes, in the heels, God knows where. Or she was taking the drugs orally. I wondered about the drugs. Certainly not cocaine. She wasn't on a high. Just an obedient zombie.

Marta came back, carrying her fur coat and a bottle of champagne. "Come on, Jasmine. We're going for a ride." Marta glanced at me. "To the Ritz, maybe. Have you ever been there?"

Jasmine dragged her head from side to side, as if she were watching a tennis match in slow motion. "Never."

Marta put a finger to her lips, kissed it, then pressed it against Jasmine's lips. "You're in for a treat. We all are."

I grabbed Jasmine by the arm. "Let's go."

Marta led the way outside, back toward the bar. Another auction had apparently been completed. The bamboo cage was empty, and the crowd was back mingling with each other. "Let's get a quick drink before we get out of here," I told Marta. "I really need one."

"Yes, you do. For a while there you had me worried. You were all up tight."

There was a stammer in my voice. "I—this is all new to me."

"A virgin," Marta said almost dreamily. "How cute."

"Get me a whiskey, will you, Marta? Make it a double."

She went toward the bar to order the drink, and I applied pressure to Jasmine's elbow. "Come with me," I said, pushing her into the crowd. The music was even louder than before, and an area in the middle of the room had been cleared for dancing. I tried to get my bearings, looking for the exit.

A tall, stoop-shouldered man reeking of gin patted my shoulder with a bony hand. "Lucky bastard," he said, staring down at Jasmine with rheumy eyes. "I never should have let you outbid me. Want to split the bill, and we'll do a double?"

"Forget it, buddy."

Oh, well." He slipped a card into my breast pocket. "Let me know how she was. Maybe I'll go higher next time."

I stood on my toes trying to spot the exit. Another hand grabbed my shoulder. "Are you trying to leave without me?" Marta demanded.

"Well, I'm the one that who paid for the merchandise. I think I'll just make it a twosome tonight, Marta."

My shoulder seemed to be a magnet for hands. This one belonged to the muscle-bound auctioneer. "You're new here, mister. If you're going to take Jasmine off the premises, you'll have to leave a deposit. A thousand pounds."

"A thousand pounds? What if Miss Howard accompanies us?"

His eyes swiveled from mine to hers.

She pursed her lips for a moment, then said: "I don't think Mr. Polo is ready for our games, Terry. Jasmine stays."

"You heard the lady," he said in a stony voice.

I shrugged and opened my palms. "Terry. That's your name, huh?"

"Yeah, that's—"

I pivoted on my hip and drove a fist, with the middle knuckle extended, into his solar plexus. He straightened up a

64

second, opened his mouth to gasp, his skin going from red to gray, then folded like a deck chair, sinking slowly to the floor. Marta screamed for help. I grabbed Jasmine by one of her ponytails and started pulling her toward where I hoped the door was located.

With the combination of people screaming and the heavy rock music I never heard them coming up behind me. I felt the blow to the back of my neck, though, a knife-sharp pain. Then my feet went on strike and I fell to my knees. The next blow was to the ribs. Luckily an elbow got in the way. Lucky for my ribs, that is. My elbow didn't appreciate it at all.

I rolled away through a sea of shoes, knocking down people like bowling pins. I took in deep breaths and struggled back to my feet in time to see one of the bartenders picking his way through the bodies and coming at me, his hands held out in front of him, palms open, fingers slightly curled in the classic pose of a karate master. I caught a quick glimpse of Marta. She had little Jasmine by one of her ponytails. Marta was smiling, like the cat that had just salted and peppered the canary.

I kept backing away, looking for some kind of help. All I saw were the seasick face of the auctioneer and two of the Adonis bartenders closing in on me from the other side, looks of victory already stitched on their faces. Three against one, the hero wounded and alone in a hostile crowd. What would Chuck Norris do? Grin through the pain and start ballet-kicking the shit out of everyone. My feet felt as if they were wearing two of Imelda Marcos's safe-deposit boxes, so scratch Norris. Sylvester Stallone would just let them keep hitting him in the head until their hands broke, but that's how he ended up talking the way he does, so scratch Stallone. Robin Williams would do his Jonathan Winters routine and sneak out while everyone was rolling on the floor in laughter. But these guys didn't look as if they had much of a sense of humor. So scratch Williams.

Wounded, outnumbered, unarmed, I used the only weapon I had left, my panic-filled voice. "It's a raid! Police! Hide the drugs! Police!" My voice didn't carry far over the music, but far enough to start a chorus of shouts from those nearby, who quickly passed the word along to the rest of the room. There were mingled screams and shouts. The most distinguishable were "Police!" and "Get the fuck out of my way!"

A mass of knees, arms, chests, and butting heads started a wave of flesh toward the exit, like thirsty cattle to a waterhole. I was lucky to stay on my feet. If anyone fell to the floor, he was in danger of being trampled to death. It was a typical panic situation, with no thought of ladies first, just a lemminglike compulsion to get out of the building. Luckily, the big exit doors opened outward. Otherwise there would have been a squashing scene reminiscent of one of those soccer-match tragedies. As it was, the crowd hit the street and struck out for places unknown.

"Unknown" was an understatement as far as I was concerned. I had no idea where I was, just that my feet were making good progress on slippery cobblestones. I zigzagged a few blocks before slowing down and looking back. No pillars of salt, just the sight of nervous men and women jumping into cars or running as fast as their dancing shoes would allow them. I couldn't see the auctioneer or the muscled bartenders. Nor Marta or little Jasmine.

I leaned against a damp wall and tried to get my breath back. Feeling was starting to come back to my neck and arms. I started hiking again, wishing I had the raincoat I'd given to Jasmine. Jasmine. What the hell was I going to do about her? What could I do? Call the cops? Tell them I had been at a slave auction and had paid for a pretty young girl who might be underage, might be on drugs, or might be a high-priced hooker putting on a hell of an act?

By now I was completely lost, and signs of life were getting thinner by the moment. Where were all those beautiful taxis? A short, burly man came into sight. He was properly bundled up for the weather in a dark duffel coat and was wearing one of those long-billed baseball-style caps that you saw on Hemingway in pictures of him deep-sea fishing.

"Listen," I told him, "I'm a bit lost, trying to find a cab."

"They don't come down here often."

I hadn't seen any of those lovely red telephone boxes either. "How about a telephone?"

He tilted the bill of his cap back. He had a couple of days

66

of gray beard on his chin and a wind-gnawed face that looked as if it had been around for at least seventy years. "Yank?" he asked.

"Right."

"Too young for the war, huh?"

"Which war?"

He snorted into his coat sleeve. "Stay right here. I'll call a cab for you."

I was huddling in a doorway, figuring that the ancient mariner had been putting me on, when the cab came into sight. "Where to?" he said gruffly as I gratefully fell into the back seat.

"The Ritz Hotel. Is it far from here?"

"Yes," he acknowledged. "More ways than one."

10

.

The flowers were the first thing I noticed when I got back to my room. A lavish bouquet of red, yellow, and purple blossoms set in a garlanded wicker basket, secreting a sweet, spicy perfume. There was a card, thick cotton bond with embossed roses on it, and the simple printed statement "Best Wishes." No signature, of course.

My stomach started churning, and I searched through the room trying to see whether my visitor had stolen anything or, worse, left something. Flowers are turning out to be one of the more reliable burglar tools. The much punier bunch of carnations I'd used to get into the back room at BeeJay's paled in comparison to the bouquet sitting on my dresser, but they'd done the job.

Not too long ago, if you wanted someone's room at a hotel, you merely had to call or approach the room clerk in person: "Mr. Polo's room number, please." And the dutiful clerk would supply you with the information. No more. Hotels now keep their guests' room numbers a closely guarded secret, to protect the guests from possible thefts or injuries and also to shield the hotels from the costly civil suits that can occur.

A recent example. One of the better hotels in San Francisco had a steady clientele of airline personnel: pilots, navigators, and stewardesses. One day a lovely young stewardess checked in. It was one of those crowded times, and the harried clerk yelled out to a bellboy, "Take Ms. X's bags to Room eleven-fourteen."

Among the crowd in the lobby was a jerk who took a look at Ms. X and liked what he saw. He gave her a few minutes to get to her room, then knocked on her door, used her name, and said there had been a mixup in her baggage. She opened the door, feeling, as she testified in her deposition, that it must be a hotel employee since he knew her name and room number. She was viciously assaulted and raped.

The jerk was caught and sentenced to twenty-three years in prison. The victim sued him, but he could never make enough license plates in twenty-three years to pay for even a small portion of her attorney's bill. But the hotel did pay, and the amount was well into six figures.

So now, if some villain wants to find out just what room his victim is staying in, he either has to follow the victim to the room or go another route. Flowers are one way. Just order a big, easily recognized bouquet from a florist near the hotel and tell them it's important that the flowers get to the right room at a certain time. "It's her birthday. I want it to be a surprise. She'll just be coming back from dinner, etc." Then wait in the lobby, watch for the delivery, and follow the bellboy on his appointed task.

Most hotels spend a fortune on rugs, furniture, paintings, those kinds of things, but tend to skimp a little on locks, because they are constantly being opened by both staff and guests. I checked my room's lock. It looked sturdy, reliable, well made. Which meant that an accomplished burglar would have to work one or two minutes to manipulate it, rather than just a few seconds.

No matter how good the lock, the sharpies find a way of manipulating it. Give a top-flight burglar five or six different room keys from the same hotel and he'll be able to make up several versions of a master key, one that will work all the hotel doors in a short time. The greedy one-hit burglars check in in groups, compare keys, use high-speed filing machines on sheets of high-tech nylon to cut the masters. The nylon isn't as strong as metal, but it doesn't have to be. It's going to open only a few doors. The fact that the nylon has a little give even makes it better in working the lock's tumblers. They'll make copies of the master and in half a day's work will knock over as many as twenty or thirty rooms.

If the burglar isn't a skilled locksmith himself he'll try and get a master key from one of the hotel maids, or at least a picture of the key, then take it to a specialist. That scam is usually worked by a couple, Mr. and Mr. Tourist, who stay a few days and get on a chummy basis with the chambermaid. Mrs. Tourist will get her to start talking about her life, her children. She'll ask for tips about where to go, where to eat, and when finally check-ing out, she'll get the chambermaid to pose for a picture. "To make our trip complete. You've been so nice." The picture is sure to have the master key in it somewhere, be it on an elastic band around her wrist or dangling on a chain from her uniform. Mr. and Mr. Tourist will leave a nice tip, then rush to get the picture developed, the negative cropped and blown up, and take it to a friendly locksmith. Then Mr. and Mrs. Tourist can check into another hotel and start the procedure all over again, mean-while looting at leisure the place they've just left.

Which is why, if you've checked into a major hotel lately, you've probably found that the room key you're given is really nothing more than a plastic credit card whose metallic computer code opens the door. As soon as your stay is finished, that card is destroyed and the hotel computer recodes the room's lock and prints up a new card. The sharpies will find a way to beat those too, so the moral is, never leave anything of value in your room.

I had no way of telling whether anyone had gone through my belongings, sparse as they were. I worked my paranoia up to the point where I was looking under the bed, into the toilet tank and even peeking into the light sockets for possible bugs. I didn't find anything, but that certainly didn't mean something wasn't there.

Who would want to bug my room or plant something that might be embarrassing or illegal? Gurbeep Singh? Why? I'd done my job. Delivered the envelope from Raymond. Marta Howard?

She'd hardly have had time to set up the flower delivery after the fiasco at the slave auction. Had she done it earlier, after I went to her apartment? I looked at the bouquet again. Maybe I had a secret admirer. It was possible. And maybe Prince Charles would ask me to take Diana to a cricket match. The odds were about the same on both.

I went to the hotel lobby and used a pay phone to call Raymond Singh in San Francisco. The phone rang a good dozen times, and I was about to hang up when Raymond's voice came over loud and clear, as if he were standing next to me in the adjoining booth.

"Yes, Raymond Singh here."

"And Nick Polo here in London, Raymond."

"Ah, Nicky. Good to hear from you. How goes the hunt?"

"The hunt is over. I found Gurbeep and gave him the envelope. He says your request will be handled as you wish. He didn't sound to happy about it."

Raymond laughed deeply. "That is his problem, Nick. You have done well. Stay over there for a couple of days. Enjoy yourself."

"You didn't happen to send some flowers to my room, did you, Raymond?"

"Flowers? I like you, Nick. But I send flowers only to beautiful women."

"Speaking of beautiful women, do you know someone named Marta Howard?"

"Sorry, Nick. Someone just came in. I've got to go. Good job. I'll see you when you get back." He severed the connection before I could say anything.

Sleep seemed to come in fifteen-minute bursts. I finally struggled out of bed a little after eight, feeling as if I'd wrestled more than my share of alligators. The thought of getting back to San Francisco cheered me up, so I was showered, shaved, dressed, and full of room-service coffee when they came to the door. Both were in their late forties, maybe early fifties. One had thick, curly black hair. The other's hair was a little gray, starting to thin in front. They were dressed in identical tan raincoats.

72

Curly flapped open a wallet at me. "Mr. Polo, I'm Chief Inspector Carter. This is Inspector Mandel."

"Scotland Yard, I presume," I said, backing away and waving them into the room.

"No," Mandel said. "Murder squad." He had a thick, heavy voice. He took out a handkerchief and gave his nose a loud honk as he looked around the room. If I was going to get the "good-guy, bad-guy" routine, Carter was apparently going to be the good guy.

"Sorry to break in on you like this, Mr. Polo, but we were hoping you wouldn't mind coming along for a little ride with us."

"Sure," I said, slowly reaching a hand into my pants pocket, extracting my old police badge, and showing it to the two London cops. It looked like a time when professional courtesy was going to come in handy.

Mandel said, "I thought you would have had to turn that in when you left the department."

So much for professional courtesy. If they knew I was an ex-policeman, they also knew that I had served six months in a federal prison. The world is just getting too small. A few telephone calls, a faxed rap sheet, and a cop halfway around the world can learn most of your secrets in a couple of hours.

"No," I said lamely. "Over there you have to buy your own badge, so when you leave you keep it."

Carter gave me a polite little smile. Mandel just stared. "You own a couple of guns, don't you?"

They had really done their homework. "Yes, but they're back home." I opened my sport coat. "You're free to check if you want."

Mandel took a step forward, but Carter stopped him by saying: "I'm sure that won't be necessary. All ready to go? I'd take a coat if I were you. It's a little chilly."

My knees got even weaker. When last seen, my coat was hanging around Jasmine's thin shoulders. Was Carter throwing a high, fast one at me? Had they found my coat, perhaps wrapped around Jasmine's body? Murder Squad. It somehow had a harsher, more brutal sound than Homicide.

"I'm fine, gentleman, but curious. Where are we going?"

"Just need your help on a case we're working on," Carter said placidly. "We'd appreciate your cooperation." He looked down at my feet. "The terrain might be a little rough. Do you have another pair of shoes?"

"No. I brought only one pair. I traveled light."

"Let's go, then," Mandel grunted.

There were dozens more questions I wanted to ask. For openers, what, or who, was it they were going to show me? How the hell had they picked my name up? And how had they known I was staying at the Ritz? You didn't have to surrender your passport in London. So who knew I was at the Ritz? Gurbeep Singh. Marta Howard. And Marta had mentioned the Ritz to Jasmine. Then there were the two private investigators I'd dealt with, Proctor and Fields. I was afraid the sound of my gurgling stomach could be heard over the humming of the elevator as we made our way to the lobby.

No shiny red Jaguar sedan for Carter and Mandel, like the one that Chief Inspector Morse drives on television, just a nondescript sedan. Mandel drove, while Carter sat in the back with me, humming a cheery tune. We all played the strong, silent type as Mandel drove through Piccadilly Circus and along the Strand, then took a series of turns, taking us into a dark, rundown part of town. I would have bet a lot of money that we were heading for the place where Marta Howard had taken me the night before. I would have lost that bet. Mandel pulled up at a grimy building of moldy gray stone. Carter held the car door open for me. "Metropolitan Police Station, Thames Division," he said, adding a moment later, "Oldest police division in all of London."

Officers in dark-blue uniforms, their white caps ribbed with a checkered black-and-white band, began snapping salutes at both Carter and Mandel. I was led into the building, which looked like police stations the world over: bare wood peeking out from under old paint, worn-down linoleum with the wood floor showing through in patches, mug shots of hard, ugly, snarling criminals tacked to the walls. They always pin up the meanest, ugliest-looking ones. If you ever have to spend some time

74

poring over mug shots, you'll be amazed at how many happy faces you see. Some people are just programmed from birth to smile at the camera.

"This way," Mandel said, putting a hard finger into my spine to usher me down the hallway, through a squeaking door, and into a room that looked like a miniature mess hall. Police officers, most in shirt sleeves, were sitting around battered, formica-topped tables. At the rear of the room a man in a white chef's hat was turning over dozens of slices of bacon on a restaurant-sized black iron stove.

"Coffee?" Carter inquired.

"Yes, thanks."

He brought over a heavy white mug, handed it to me, and said: "Have a seat. Be with you in a minute."

I sat on a bench seat across from a burly-looking, shirt-sleeved officer still wearing his cap. He dropped his newspaper just low enough to give me a quick glance. Years of police training must have taught him to analyze people in seconds. Properly figuring I was a nobody, he went right back to reading his paper.

The delicious smell of the frying bacon almost made up for the bitter coffee. Other officers, male and female, came and went, going up to the counter in front of the stove, coming back with plates piled high with fried potatoes, scrambled eggs, and fragrant bacon slices.

The man across from me was apparently through with his paper. He gave me a heavy look. "I'm an ex–San Francisco policeman," I told him, hoping to drum up a conversation and possibly pump him about any recent murder victims. "Do you guys eat your meals here when you're on duty?"

"Right," he said, after considering the question for a few seconds.

"Each station has its own restaurant?"

"Canteen," he corrected me. "Sure. Every station has a canteen."

"Canteen." It was one of those words that the English use so well. "Canteen" made me think of World War II movies in which impossibly beautiful Hollywood stars tried to look like waitresses while serving coffee and donuts to regular GI Joes.

"You don't have canteens back in San Francisco?" he asked, putting a couple of extra syllables into "Francisco."

"No."

"Where do the men eat?"

"At restaurants on their beats."

He shook his head, not liking the sound of it, and went back to his paper.

Different worlds. More than just a language barrier. I knew a few San Francisco beat men who hadn't missed a restaurant meal in years. They would literally put on their uniforms on their days off and come into town for a meal. Not because they were cheap. Because they were spoiled. Home cooking just couldn't match the kitchens of the city's top restaurants.

The beat was their territory, and if another cop from another beat did any poaching he was asking for trouble.

The restaurants were happy to have an officer on the scene, considering it cheap hold-up and burglar insurance, so they'd feed the beat cop, sometimes right in the kitchen, try out new dishes on him. One guy became such a gourmet that when he retired he was hired as a food critic for one of the local papers.

Carter came to the door, peeked in, and gave me a "come here" wave of his right arm. He led me out of the building, down a wobbly, bare wooden boat ramp, and onto a police cutter, maybe thirty feet in length, black-bottomed, the wheelhouse milk-white, the gray water of the Thames burbling against its sleek hull. There was a checkered band around the boat's cabin, exactly matching those around the caps of the two uniformed policeman who helped me on board. One of the uniformed men undid the mooring ropes, and we throttled away from the pier.

Carter disappeared into the cabin, coming back in a couple of minutes with a heavy canvas pea jacket. "Better put this on," he said seriously. "Wouldn't want you catching pneumonia." It was pneumonia-catching weather. The skies were an ominous gun-metal gray, and the wind was kicking up the murky gray-green water. The boat's diesel engine emitted thick, pungent fumes into the air, overpowering the smell of the river itself. "I hope you don't get seasick," said Carter.

"Me too," I said, spreading my feet as the little boat rocked in the wake of a passing tug towing a barge loaded with the rusty, rotting carcasses of crushed automobiles. "Not much traffic out here," I said to Carter, trying to get him to enlarge his role of good cop. Carter looked as if he were waging a small inner battle with himself as to whether or not to talk to me. Departmental pride won out. "Metropolitan Police. Almost joined up myself. They patrol fifty-four miles of the river, from up at Staines, past the barriers, and out to Dartford Creek. Started in 1790 by the West India Company. The first uniformed police department in the world, approved by the government, of course, but paid for by the merchant companies. Tough times on the river then." He inhaled deeply, eyes roaming the Thames. "Sailing man myself."

"I used to work the crab-fishing boats in San Francisco for my uncle when I was a kid."

That raised his eyebrows a bit. "Really?"

We swapped boat stories for a few minutes, then passed under a gray concrete bridge.

"That was London Bridge. New London Bridge. There have been several. You know the old nursery rhyme, "London Bridge is falling down." Well, a few of them did. This one went up in 1967. Some of your people bought the old one, dismantled it, and sent it out to some place in America. Arizona, I think."

"You think right, though I don't know what they were thinking of when they bought it."

Carter laughed heartily and pointed toward the bow of the boat. "The rumor is that the Americans bought the wrong bridge. That's the one they thought they were buying."

Dead ahead was the magnificent Tower Bridge, its twin towers looking like beautiful, narrow castles.

"Bought the wrong bridge," Carter repeated, grinning from ear to ear, so I dutifully gave him a polite laugh.

Carter turned tourist guide, pointing to a huge warship he identified as the *Belfast*. Almost directly across from the *Belfast* was the Tower of London itself, an imposing square structure with magnificent turrets and towers of grimy beige stone.

77

"Looks as if Basil Rathbone and Errol Flynn should be hacking away at each other with sabers while trying to get to the drawbridge, doesn't it?" I asked Carter.

"Hmmmmmm" was his only response.

Once we were under Tower Bridge, Carter retreated to the boat's cabin. The wind kicked up, and I had to sit down to keep from falling down. The warm, cozy-looking cabin looked off-limits to civilians. Every once in a while Carter or Mandel or one of the uniformed officers would take a peek out at me, usually over the rim of a steaming coffee mug.

The river widened out, and there were a lot of rotting piers and old wrecks of buildings being torn down and new condominium-style apartment houses going up. The boat slowed down and turned starboard toward the shore, docking at what looked like the wharf of an old, abandoned shipyard.

More uniformed officers were waiting at the dock to help with the mooring lines. Carter and Mandel ignored me while talking to the officers. Then Carter gave me another of his "get over here" waves. We went up a rickety pier, past stacks of ragged pieces of rusting metal, coils of wire cable, and stripped-down machines that looked as if they once could have been lathes.

Mandel kept glancing over his shoulder to make sure I was keeping up the pace. We left the pier and turned right along a black, moss-covered sea wall, then up a sandy knoll to a group of men, all dressed in civilian clothes, all wearing raincoats. Two of them had large, expensive-looking cameras in their hands. They were standing around, shaking their arms, moving their feet up and down in the sand to keep warm. A group of professionals who had done their job and were waiting for the signal so they could get out of there and back to their nice, warm offices or laboratories.

Mandel and Carter waded into the group and started asking questions, then giving orders. It was Mandel who gave me the wave this time. "Mr. Polo, would you mind coming over here? Walk that way, please."

"That way" was over a stretch of sand that the tides had swept clean. I walked around a group of aluminum packing cases. Then Mandel waved me to a stainless-steel hospital gurney. The body was covered with gray blankets. "Know this man?" Carter asked, jerking the blanket down with a snap.

I didn't know whether to be relieved or sick. The pasty face of Ronnie, the clerk at BeeJay's, stared back at me with the glassy-eyed look that only the recently dead have. His red-black hair was tangled together like discarded New Year's confetti. A wound coated with coagulated blood lay in the middle of his toast-rack-thin chest.

"Don't really know him, Chief Inspector. Met him once."

"Just once?" Mandel boomed. "His name is Ronald Heston. He had your business card, with your hotel's name written on the back, rolled up and hidden in the lining of his jacket."

It was a chore to keep the fear from showing on my face. I had actually seen him twice at BeeJay's, once when I gave him the sealed Ritz Hotel envelope with my business card along with a copy of the cashier's check, the second time when I used the carnations to get to the back of the shop. "It's a long story," I said. "Can we go somewhere a little bit warmer and discuss it?"

On the way back to the boat I saw why Carter was so curious about the number of shoes I owned. One of his men was starting to make plaster casts of my footsteps in the sand.

11

.

The boat ride back to the police station was a repeat of the
earlier trip, me standing outside and listening to my teeth chatter
while Carter and Mandel huddled inside with the crew. I was
hustled off the boat and back into the station wagon. The drive
didn't last long enough for the car's heater to do any good.

Mandel pulled through one of the arches of yet another old
gray stone building, into a brick courtyard. They kept me in the
middle this time, Carter leading the way, Mandel nipping at my
heels. Up an outer metal stairway, through a door opening onto
a narrow hallway, and finally into a small room containing a
single table and several folding metal chairs. No windows. No
paintings. No mirrors. No calendars. It was not designed to
make you feel comfortable.

"Be right back," Carter said, and both men trooped out.
The hard, clicking sound of the lock falling into place told me
that if I tried the doorknob all I'd get was some exercise for my
wrist.

I killed time trying to decipher the scratchings on the ta-
bletop. Lots of names and initials. The only thing different from
the tables back in San Francisco was that the word "fuck" didn't

show up as often. It was almost an hour before Carter and Mandel came back. Mandel's gloomy face cheered me up.

"The shoe castings didn't match, huh?" I asked.

Mandel settled into the chair across from me. His rugged features remained calm, but there was disappointment etched in the lines around his mouth and between his eyes. "Could have two pairs, Polo," he finally said. "We've only your word that you just have the one."

"And you've already checked my room, haven't you?"

There was a knock on the door and a young man in a red sweater, elbows poking through the sleeves, came in carrying an enamel tray with a pot of coffee and a stack of sandwiches. He nodded at me while passing out the food, then left without a word.

Carter added sugar to his coffee, stirring slowly as if he were mixing an explosive formula. I took a sip from my cup and figured that he might well be doing just that. "Tell me," Carter said after sampling his brew, "about your time in prison. Must have been hard time for a police officer, eh?"

"I don't think there's any such thing as good time, Chief Inspector."

"What they get you for?" Mandel, ever the bad guy, asked bluntly.

There are times when you're backed into a corner, when most of your usual ploys just don't work, so you have to rely on that much-abused ingredient the truth. "It was a year or so after I left the police department," I told them. "I was working as a private investigator for an attorney. He hired me to find a client whom he was representing on drug charges. I found him in a motel room, dead from sampling too much of his own product. There was just one suitcase in the room. It was filled with cash. I took it back to the attorney and we decided to keep the money, split it down the middle. A quarter of a million dollars each. A couple of weeks later the attorney got nervous. His client's partners figured he had the money. He made a deal with the cops. I went to prison. He didn't."

Mandel picked up one of the sandwiches, peeled back the

top slice of bread, wrinkled his nose, and dropped the mess back onto the tray. "This was after you left the force?"

"Right."

Mandel glared into his coffee mug. "What did they catch you doing while you were a copper? More drug money?"

"No. I just quit. I inherited a little money when my parents died." I waited until Mandel pulled his eyes from the coffee and stared into mine. "The job just wasn't fun anymore, Inspector." His eyes held mine for several seconds. Then he gave me a slight nod. It was an answer he could live with, an answer only another cop, no matter what country he lived and worked in, would understand.

"What happened to your inheritance?" inquired Carter, who wasn't put off by whatever it was that Mandel had found in the sandwiches. He took a big bite. Then, while chewing away, he added, "What made you become a private investigator?"

"Bad investments. I put the money I'd inherited in the stock market rather than on the horses. I had to go to work."

"And your work took you all the way to London," Mandel said pointedly.

I gave them the whole story. Most of it, anyway. Neither man bothered to make notes, which meant that the conversation was being recorded.

When I told them about how Raymond Singh had hired me, Carter stirred in his chair as if to relieve a muscle cramp. "All that money to deliver a package to a man," he said.

"A microcassette, a letter, and a check. I saw them put into the envelope. That's all there was. No drugs. No jewels."

"What was the amount of the check?" Carter asked.

"Sixty thousand American dollars."

Mandel snorted his disbelief. "And the man you were delivering the, ah, envelope to?"

"Gurbeep Singh. A cousin of Raymond's. Distant cousin, is the way he described him." Carter and Mandel exchanged glances and small shrugs. Gurbeep Singh was a name that didn't click with either of them.

Mandel put both elbows on the table, threading a pencil through his fingers. "And where did you make the delivery?"

"At Blackwell's. Last night."

Carter reached for another of the sandwiches. "Blackwell's? The casino?"

"Right."

Carter gave another snort. "You arranged to meet him there?"

"No, I just sort of ran into him." I reached into my pocket and pulled out the photograph of Raymond and Gurbeep Singh. "That's Gurbeep on the right. Raymond gave me the photograph so I'd know what he looked like."

Both men took their time examining the picture. Then Carter asked, "Interesting, but tell us now: Just how did Ronald Heston come to have your business card with the name of your hotel?"

"Raymond Singh told me that Gurbeep Singh operated a store on Carnaby Street, BeeJay's. I went there. Singh wasn't in. I left my card with the store clerk. He had a name tag that said "Ronnie." I saw him at the store, not once but twice, now that I think of it, then on the beach this morning. Nowhere else."

Mandel picked up the photograph, flicking a thumbnail against the edge. "Then Ronnie told you where to find this Gurbeep Singh?"

Now we came down to nitty-gritty time. Back home I'd just have kept my mouth shut and waited until I had an attorney sitting beside me before I answered one single question. Here I was lost. I didn't even know the difference between a solicitor and a barrister, though I thought that Rumpole was one of the latter and got to wear one of those silly wigs while defending his all-too-often guilty clients. I stalled by sipping coffee and biting into one of the sandwiches.

"No," I eventually said, manfully swallowing whatever was between the slices of stale white bread. "I found out that the listed owner of the store was a Marta Howard. I followed her to the Royal Opera, where she met Gurbeep Singh, then to Blackwell's."

Carter was no fool and jumped on the obvious opening. "Found out Marta Howard was the owner of the store? Just

84

how did you do that? Did Mr. Heston supply you with this information?"

"No." I looked at the sandwich in my hand for a moment, then gave up, dropping it on the table. "I hired a private investigator. A Mr. George Proctor. He checked public records and found that the store was operated by a company called Carlisle, Inc. Marta Howard's name was listed on the license."

Mandel's face broke into a 'I just won the lottery' smile.

"Georgie Proctor. You kidding me?"

"No."

Mandel couldn't stop smiling. "Georgie Proctor. How did you ever get hooked up with that bugger?"

"The phone book," I admitted sheepishly.

"Georgie Proctor," Mandel repeated, slapping his hands on his thighs. "Bet he gave you a thorough screwing, didn't he?"

"Thorough," I agreed. "I take it you know Proctor well."

"Worked for the department once," Carter said in an amused tone. "File clerk. Hear him tell it, he was running Scotland Yard." Bad news. Carter and Mandel would talk to Proctor, and he'd tell them everything. Including the fact that he'd given me only Marta Howard's name, not her address.

Mandel tapped his pencil against the table in a nervous rhythm. "So Georgie sicced you onto this Howard woman and she led you to Singh."

I didn't want to get the other private investigator, William Shields, in trouble unless I had to. "Proctor gave me her name. I went back to BeeJay's a second time. Ronnie was still there, working alone behind the counter. There was an envelope on the counter with Marta Howard's name and address on it."

Carter questioned me about the dates and times of my visits to BeeJay's, then asked, "What did you do next?"

Back to nitty-gritty time. "How was Ronnie killed?"

Carter made a jabbing motion with his right hand. "Knife blade in the heart."

My mind went immediately to Howard's chauffeur and his Philippine butterfly knife. "I checked out Carlisle, Inc. There was an address listed, 25 the Holtons, in Kensington. I went over there. A big, tough-looking guy first told me he was Gurbeep

Singh. When I challenged him on that, he got nasty. Pulled out a knife. Chased me out of there."

"Did Georgie Proctor give you this address in Kensington?" Carter asked quickly.

"No. I had one of those computer database information centers in the United States run the name."

"And they gave it to you, just like that?" asked Mandel.

"Almost anything that's public information worldwide is stored in their database," I said, which was more or less the truth. The kind of information that my money man in Southern California hacked into wasn't, and I saw no need to supply the London cops with those other exotic names that my source had supplied me. He'd said that there was a yellow tag on Carlisle, Inc.'s, bank account, so if they looked hard enough, they'd find the other police agency that was interested in Carlisle.

Carter asked more detailed questions about the man with the knife: height, weight, age, that kind of thing. "When I waited for Marta Howard to come out of her apartment last night, the same guy, the one with the knife, came over in a Daimler and picked her up. Drove her to the Royal Opera."

"And you're sure it was the same man?" Carter asked, draining his coffee cup.

"Definitely."

We went over the story a couple more times, and I thought I was safely out of there. But Carter did the Columbo trick, going to the door, then asking: "Just one more question, Mr. Polo. When you delivered your envelope to Mr. Singh, what time was that?"

"A little after midnight, I think."

"And what did you do then?"

"We had a drink together. Singh wanted to stay and do some more gambling. Marta Howard wanted to go out and dance. We went to some nightclub. I don't know the name of it."

"And you took her home later?"

"No. We left separately."

"Was she in the Daimler?"

"No. We took a cab to the nightclub. I took a cab home."

"And you didn't see the gentleman with the knife again?"

"Not after he dropped Marta Howard off at the Royal Opera."

Carter nodded solemnly, then went out the door. Next it was Mandel's time to play Columbo. "Oh, one more question," he said in light tone. "May I have your passport?"

12

.

The bobby was right out of central casting: tall, handsome, standing erect with his hands clasped behind him, dimpled chin under his cap's strap. He gave Carter and Mandel a crisp military salute, nearly clicking his heels together as he said, "Afternoon, sir."

Carter gave him a brief nod, then turned to me. "You are sure this is the right place?"

"This is it," I said, looking at the white facade of 25 the Holtons.

Mandel got into a hushed conversation with the bobby. Chief Inspector Carter lumbered toward the front door, with me following in his wake. The door was wide open. Light streaming in from the drawn curtains drew striped patterns on the scuffed hardwood floor.

"This is where you met the man who claimed to be Gurbeep Singh?" Carter asked, his eyes slowly surveying the room as if he were a painter getting ready to give an estimate.

"Right," I said. "The guy who drove Marta Howard around in the Daimler."

Carter's neck craned up to the ceiling. "And you didn't go into any of the other rooms?"

"No, he pulled a knife and I took off."

Carter grunted something that I couldn't understand, which was probably just as well under the circumstances.

"Tell me about the woman who answered the door," he said.

"Very short, in her sixties at least, appeared to be East Indian. She went through that door over there. A few minutes later the man came out to see me."

"This door?" Carter asked, striding purposefully toward the door at the far end of the room.

"Right."

"And you say you saw a couple of small children as the old woman went out through the doorway?"

"Yes, young kids. Six or seven years of age, something like that."

"How were they dressed?" Carter asked, pushing the door open with the heel of his hand.

"I didn't get much of a look at them, Chief Inspector."

"But you're sure they were both young children, eh?"

"Yes, I'm sure of that."

Carter pushed the door all the way open, stopping briefly to check its lock. The same neglected hardwood flooring continued on through two large rooms, bare of furniture except for folding metal chairs and matching large-projection TV sets in both rooms. The faded cream walls were covered with children's crayon drawings of replicas of cars, boats, and stick-figure boys and girls. The floors were littered with overlapping magazines and video cassettes, some in their boxes, others stacked haphazardly in piles of threes and fours.

Ashtrays overflowing with cigarette and cigar butts were scattered about. There were numerous burn marks on the floor, reminding me of the advice of an always angry army sergeant when one of his men would ask where an ashtray was. "You're standing on it, asshole" was his stock reply.

Carter bent over to check out the magazines, and I followed suit. There was an equal mixture of children's coloring books, comics, and adult hardcore magazines. In one stack of cassettes I saw a copy of *The Little Mermaid* sandwiched between *Insatiable*

Sex Goddesses and *Naked Meatpackers,* a triple bill I'm sure Mr. Disney would not have approved of.

"Disgusting crap," Carter said loudly as he began punching buttons on one of the televisions. The screen went through a kaleidoscope of colors as the sounds of someone grunting loudly over a symphony of violins filled the room. As the screen came into focus, the bulky figures of two fat, middle-aged men filled the screen. The camera moved around jerkily and one of the men looked directly into the lens, nodded his head, and reached down and pulled the hair back from the young woman's face so that the viewer could better observe her mouth devouring his penis. The girl's doe eyes moved lazily toward the camera and I tried to keep the cringe from showing on my face as I recognized little Jasmine. Carter punched the off button, his voice papery dry as he expressed his opinion. "Those two bastards should have their balls chopped off. The girl can't be more than fifteen years old."

I followed Carter's lead into a kitchen that smelled of spices and cooking grease. There were plates with portions of cold, congealing food and glasses half-filled with milk lying on top of a large oak table. The kitchen sink was filled to the top with dirty dishes, the countertops littered with more of the same. "Didn't spend much time doing housework, did they?" Carter said with a wrinkling of his nose.

A staircase, its banister graffitied with crayon doodlings, led up to the second floor. The hallway was covered with more of the crayon art, none reaching above three feet or so. There were a half-dozen bedrooms, all in total disarray, multicolored clothing cascading out of open bureau drawers. The closets were empty except for rows of metal clothes hangers and dust balls. Sour-smelling piles of dirty laundry were all over the place. There were three bathrooms, all in as bad a mess as the bedrooms.

"Well, what do you think, Mr. Polo? Looks like your friends left in a bit of a hurry, doesn't it?"

"They were no friends of mine, Chief Inspector."

He glared at me with one of his x-ray stares. "But they were friends of your client, Mr. Raymond Singh, weren't they?"

91

"Beats me. Did you check out the store, BeeJay's?"

"Closed and locked."

"What about Marta Howard's apartment?"

"No one there, Mr. Polo," Carter said, stalking off toward the stairway. We found Mandel in one of the TV rooms downstairs, sifting through the magazines and videocassettes. "Nothing worthwhile upstairs," Carter said.

Mandel held up one of the magazines. There was a picture of a girl tied upside down to a wooden cross. "You've seen these?"

"Yes. Let's get some fresh air," Carter said, sticking his hands in his suit-coat pockets and marching stiff-shouldered toward the front door. The exhaust-filled air outside could not really be classified as "fresh," but compared to what was circulating around inside 25 the Holtons I felt as if I were suddenly inhaling pure oxygen.

Carter and Mandel went into a huddle with the bobby, and I strode over to the car, leaning my hands on the roof and stretching my muscles. Mandel came over to me after a few minutes. "You can find your way back to the hotel from here," he said flatly.

"Yes, I can. How about my passport?"

"Anxious to go home, Polo?"

"Is there some reason I can't leave, Inspector Mandel?"

He made a clucking sound with his tongue. "There are a few more questions we have for you. Call me about the passport tomorrow," he replied, swiveling on his heel and heading toward Chief Inspector Carter.

"I'm checking out of the Ritz," I said to his back.

Mandel did an abrupt about-face. "Why's that?"

"I don't think I can justify another night there on my expense account," I told him, holding back the fact that the real reason was that I was sure someone had searched the room and possibly planted a bug. If they had gotten in once, they could certainly do it again.

"Wait right here," Mandel ordered.

I went back to my stretching exercises while he conferred with Carter. Carter came back alone this time. "What's this about your leaving the Ritz?" he asked harshly, a scowl on his face.

"Can't afford it anymore."

He raised an eyebrow. "Just where are you thinking of moving to?"

"Haven't got a clue. Any suggestions?"

His face softened a bit. "Yes, I do. Try the Fanning, on Bow Street. Tell them I suggested it to you." He spelled out the name to make sure I got it right, then waved an index finger under my nose. "And Polo, if you don't check into the Fanning, I damn well want to know just where you are."

13.

I somehow got the impression that Chief Inspector Carter was preparing me for a stay in one of the queen's jails by putting me into the Fanning Hotel. It had a quaint Tudor look about it on the outside: whitewashed stucco outlined in burnt-umber planking and empty flower boxes under diamond-paned windows. It was once you got through the front door—a chore in itself, since it was not wide enough for both you and your luggage—that the bloom came off the rose.

A threadbare rug ran down a hallway as narrow as the entranceway. To the right was a lounge area, with overstuffed chairs and a matching sofa facing a small bar with upturned liquor bottles nesting in those mechanical dispensers that emit half a gill and not a drop more of their precious cargoes. Off to the left, a long-jawed chap with a receding hairline and craggy eyebrows sat behind a counter watching a television set. His eyes barely left the screen when I gave him my name.

"I called ahead for a reservation," I said loud enough to be heard over the TV, which was showing some type of game show.

"Ummmhmmmm," he said, tapping a finger on the registration book.

After I signed in he handed me my room key, an old-fashioned ward key attached to a piece of green plastic the size of a dessert plate. "Room four, down the hall," the clerk said dismissively. A wide-shouldered man carrying two bulging suitcases confronted me in the hallway, and we jostled briefly like knights on horseback as we struggled by each other in the narrow confines.

Certain words express their meanings perfectly. Like "banana." If you suddenly had the opportunity to rename that noble fruit, could you come up with anything better than the original? "Shark": a sharp, dangerous word, well befitting its namesake. The English have the definitive word to describe my room at the Fanning Hotel: tacky. Dark green walls, a ceiling that once was either white or cream but now was a sickly yellow, twin beds covered with brown corduroy bedspreads, a walnut dresser that didn't match the nightstands, and a television set with one of its rabbit-ear antenna arms broken off at the midpoint. A painting of a somber-looking gentleman in a red velvet suit, holding a Boston terrier on his lap, hung on the wall between the beds.

I unpacked quickly, dropped my room key off at the counter, and ventured outside, wondering what to do with myself while waiting for Carter or Mandel to give me back my passport. I got out my London Street map and saw that I was just a couple of blocks from Covent Garden and the Royal Opera, which meant very near Blackwell's.

There was a pub down the alley from the hotel, so I had a sandwich and a beer and started plotting. The best thing to do was just sit tight, wait for the police to call, beg for my passport, and get out of the country. I didn't mind sitting tight, but not in that depressing hotel room. I was digging through my jacket pockets, looking for change, when I came across a business card:

Noel Harvey, Dental Surgeon. FDS RCPS BDS
LDS RCS.
222 Whitechapel High Street, London.
Hours 8:45–5:45.

Where had I picked up the card? What did all of those impressive letters stand for? And why couldn't Harvey work from nine to six? I drained the last of the thick beer and ordered another to get my juices flowing. I backtracked through my last few days, stopping suddenly at the auctioning of little Jasmine. A drunk had wanted to split my auction bid and join in on the fun. He had slipped his card in my pocket. A dentist, of all things. I felt a pang of remorse for his patients, feeling certain that most of them would not want a man who went to slave auctions sticking his fingers into their mouths.

Getting from where I was to Whitechapel High Street looked very simple on the map, probably no more than a two-mile hike. I turned it into an adventure by making my virgin trip on the underground, also called the tube. If you're a people-watcher, riding the tube is as good as going to a racetrack. I mean, you really see some interesting folks, a few of whom will take the time to tell you just what tiled hallway to walk down to catch the right train to get you to your destination. I made a few rookie mistakes, transferring to the wrong line, but finally ended up at the Aldgate East station, which spilled me and my fellow passengers out very near the intersection of Whitechapel and, of all places, Middlesex Street.

Harvey's office was on the street floor of a narrow, six-story medical building. A half-dozen patients were sitting in chrome and black imitation leather office chairs, listlessly turning the pages of old magazines. His receptionist was a pleasant-faced young woman in her thirties dressed in a heavily starched white nurse's uniform.

"I'd like to see Dr. Harvey," I told her, keeping my face stern and handing her one of my business cards.

Her eyebrows crept up as she read the card. "A private investigator? From America?"

"Right. I'll take only a few minutes of the doctor's time."

She had the smooth, pale skin of a nun, and there was a no-nonsense look about her eyes. "Exactly what is this all about?" she said, her voice determined.

"Just something the doctor can help me with. Tell him it's about an auction."

Her eyebrows went back into their climbing routine. "Auction?"

"He'll know what I'm talking about," I advised her.

She gave me an appraising glance, the look on her face showing she wasn't very happy with the final appraisal, then told me to wait. "I'll speak with Dr. Harvey about this." It didn't take long. A few minutes later she came out and ushered me past the waiting patients, who glanced up from their magazines long enough to give me hostile looks for cutting in front of them, through a door, down a corridor, and into a vacant room. "Wait right here. Dr. Harvey will be with you in a moment."

The room was equipped with the usual array of dental equipment: a padded chair, a spit sink, an enamel-armed drilling machine, and a tray holding all the tools needed for a modern torture chamber. The door was flung open and Dr. Harvey, all six feet three of him, marched into the room. He closed the door behind him, thrust his hands in his smock's pockets, leaving the thumbs hooked outside the way the British aristocracy do when they're posing for portraits, squared his shoulders, and in a somber voice said: "See here. What's this all about?"

"Don't you remember me, Doc? At the auction. I was the high bidder for the girl, Jasmine. You wanted to split the bill. Go halves on the fun."

Harvey opened his eyes in mock surprise. "My dear man, what are you talking about? I don't see—"

"Doc, look, I'm not trying to shake you down. Maybe you were too drunk to remember talking to me. But you were there. A beautiful young girl was auctioned off to the highest bidder. She was in a cage, remember? Then there was some confusion. People thought the police were coming. Everyone ran out into the street. Does that help your memory?"

His shoulders started to sag forward. "Don't remember anything of the kind. How did you get my name?"

I took out his business card. "You gave this to me, Doc. When you tried to buy in on the girl."

Harvey pulled his hands from his pockets and massaged his face briskly. "I—I remember going out to a club, but I don't have any recollection of—"

98

"What's the name of the club, Doctor?"

He peeked at me through his fingers. "You claim you were at this place, and you don't know the name?"

"A friend took me there."

"You're a private investigator? Is that right?"

"Yes, Doctor. I don't want to involve you in this, and I want to settle it myself, without going to the police."

At the sound of "police" his spine stiffened up. "Just what do you want from me?"

"The name and address of the club. That's all."

Harvey walked over to the dental chair, placing his hands on the padded headrest. "The Helot Club," he said softly.

"Helot?"

"Yes." He spelled it for me. "A helot was a slave in ancient Sparta."

"Just where is the club?"

The question seemed to surprise him. "Where? Well, they move it all the time. Never in the same place more than twice. You have to call, see where the auction party will be." He paused a moment before adding, "Worried about the police, I guess."

"Aren't we all? What number do you call?"

"Can't remember, really. It's in the *Fescennine*."

"The what?"

Harvey gave me another spelling lesson. "*Fescennine*. It's a paper. You can buy it at adult bookstores. The Helot Club has an ad, with a number. The number's always changing, so you have to keep buying the damn paper."

"Do you know who runs the Helot Club?"

"Not a clue," Harvey said, confidence pouring back into his voice now that he knew how little I knew. The voice grew wary again. "You're not going to bring the police into this, then, are you?"

"I hope not. Thanks for your time, Doctor."

I was halfway out the door when Harvey called me back. "How was she?" he asked in a husky voice, a smile curling his lips. It was a smirky, iniquitous smile, the kind some people get when they watch a boxer first bloody his opponent. The kind of smile a rapist gets when he knows the police don't have enough evidence to convict him. A dirty smile. The kind you want to wipe off with your fist.

"She was young, doctor. Too young for me, for you, or for anyone else at the Helot Club. If I do end up going to the police on this, do you want them to contact you here, or at your home?"

14

.

The *Fescennine* was a twelve-page specialty paper catering to the full spectrum of perverts. There were sections for straights, gays, water sports, animal lovers, bisexuals, trisexuals, transvestites, infantiles, leather specialists, rubber enthusiasts, and just plain old models and massages. My favorite was an ad for someone named Rhonda in the massage column. "Don't let your meat loaf!" her ad exclaimed in bold print.

I let out a chuckle, drawing a withering look from the well-dressed gentleman sitting next to me. His eyes darted from mine to the paper several times. Then he leaned as far away as space would permit, which wasn't very far. I was sitting at a counter seat in a small, creamery-style restaurant near the great food halls in Harrods department store, indulging in a slice of unbelievably rich cheesecake and a cup of tea, my first cup of tea since coming to London. It was something that had to be done, both the tea and visiting Harrods. The tea was very good, and so was Harrods. I hadn't been the least bit hungry until I roamed those tile-walled, rococo-ceilinged food halls, my eyes feasting upon a truly dazzling display of what seemed to be every possible variety of food. Fish: big ones, small ones, red ones, blue ones, silvery ones, popeyed, mouths open, glowing iridescently against mounds of shaved ice, shellfish, crabs, gigantic lobsters, oysters, clams ranging from coin-sized to one resembling a football. Poultry: giant turkeys, finger-sized quail, and everything in between, some cooked to golden crispness, others dangling down from hooks, their freshly plucked skin the color of wallpaper paste. Rows upon rows of neatly stacked sausages and pâtes, chocolates, and multitextured breads, and a kaleidoscope of cakes, pies, and pastries almost to pretty to eat. Almost. I spooned up another piece of the cheesecake and went back to the *Fescennine* ads, finding the Helot Club listed under "Adult Parties." Just the name and a telephone number. I jotted down the number on a piece of the Ritz Hotel's stationery. I'd taken a tablet as a souvenir, barely avoiding the temptation of jamming a couple of their magnificent towels into my luggage.

While I was paying for the tea and cake I noticed my snobby counter companion snatch up *Fescennine* and quietly slip it into his shopping bag.

I was juggling two green-and-gold Harrods' shopping bags myself, picking up gifts for friends back in San Francisco and another raincoat for myself, this time being seduced by the friendly salesman into upgrading all the way to a Burberry trench coat full of buttons, flaps, and hand grenade-clips. I used one of the department store's pay phones to try the Helot Club's number: disconnected.

I cabbed it back to the Fanning Hotel. Chief Inspector Carter and Chief Mandel were waiting for me in the lounge. They didn't look happy. I don't know exactly where they took me, but it was within sight and sound of Big Ben. It was quite dark out by now. I was hustled through a door, past a soldier in camouflage fatigues standing guard, an Uzi-type machine gun clasped in his hands.

Carter and Mandel were in a big hurry, Mandel pumping his elbows as if he were Professor Harold Hill leading a chorus of "Seventy-six Trombones." They kept me between them, so I had no choice but to keep up. Into an elevator, up to the sixth floor, down a deserted corridor, and finally through a door numbered 614, with the letters MVD neatly stenciled below the numbers, and straight through a large, deserted office with ten or more desks. Then Carter knocked on an unmarked door, and waited until he heard someone say, "Come ahead." He opened the door and Mandel placed a big hand on my back and gently nudged me through.

It was a big room with dark, Jacobean wood paneling under a white coffered ceiling. A man of medium height walked over from behind an impressive Renaissance-style desk, hand out, and said: "Ah, Mr. Polo. Thanks for coming."

His handshake was hard, matching his gray eyes. He was a handsome, lean-faced man with one side of his mouth hooked into a slight, perpetual half-smile, as if permanently amused by the world and its inhabitants. He was wearing a well-tailored chalk-striped blue suit, a wing-collared blue shirt, and a pale-gray silk tie. An expensive package.

"Turner's the name, Clive Turner." He waved a hand. "Take a seat, Mr. Polo. Get comfortable. We have lots to talk about."

"Before I sit down and we talk about anything, Mr. Turner, let's set some ground rules. Just who are you, and why should I say anything? I'm getting a little tired of being shoved around by London's finest here."

Turner glanced at Carter. "Have you been mistreating Mr. Polo, Chief Inspector?"

"No, sir. Not at all."

"They took my passport," I said.

Turner cocked his head slightly to one side.

Carter coughed into his fist, then reached into his coat pocket, pulled out a passport, and handed it to Turner, who studied it briefly and said, "You don't do a lot of traveling, do you, Mr. Polo?"

"Not as much as I'd like. In fact, I'd like to go home now."

"Yes, certainly. I can understand that." Turner laid the passport down on his desk. Apart from the passport, there was just one telephone and a gold-plated pen in an onyx base on its polished surface. "We were just hoping you could give us a bit of a hand before you return to San Francisco." He walked back behind the massive desk, plopping down into a high-backed wing chair covered in burnished bottle-green leather and decorated with brass studs. I settled into a Windsor chair as hard as marble. Carter and Mandel dutifully took up positions on each side of me.

"I still don't know who you are." I told Turner.

"Yes, yes, sorry about that. Didn't properly introduce myself, did I? I'm with MVD, Migration and Visa Department," he explained, "part of the foreign office." He leaned back in his chair, smoothed his tie, and examined both ends to see that they matched in length. "Chief Inspector Carter and Inspector Mandel have been cooperating with us on this." His eyes drifted up to mine and wandered over to the passport on his desk, then back to me. "If we all cooperate, maybe we'll get what we all want."

I was getting the impression that Clive Turner was in love with his own voice. He had the deep baritone of a preacher who keeps the front pews awake by sheer volume alone. "What do you want from me?" I asked bluntly.

He leaned forward in his chair and planted his hands knuckles down, on the desk. "Illegal immigrants, Mr. Polo. They come here from the East. Some stay, others don't. They go west. Canada. Into the States." I had a feeling Turner would have been more comfortable saying, "Into the colonies."

"And you think that I know something that can help you?"

"Yes, yes, we do." He opened a desk drawer and pulled out a large, flat envelope, opened it, and shook loose several photographs. He arranged them in a neat stack, then fanned them like a gambler getting ready to deal a blackjack hand. "Recognize any of these people?"

There were seven pictures in all. Four were mug shots, the other three taken when the men were either walking down a street or getting out of a car. One of the men walking down the street looked very familiar. "This one," I said, handing Turner the picture. Both Carter and Mandel edged up to the desk to get a look. I turned to Carter. "That's the man I met at 25 the Holtons."

"You're sure?" asked Turner.

"That's not a face you're likely to forget," I said.

Turner gave a quick smile. "Yes. Ugly brute, isn't he? Know his name?"

"He told me he was Gurbeep Singh. I knew he wasn't. He pulled a knife on me, and I left."

"Well, he was half-right," Turner said. "He uses the name Hardev Singh, as well as many others. Tell me about your meeting with this gentleman. Tell me the whole story." I went over it all, everything I'd told Carter and Mandel, hoping I hadn't left anything out or, worse, added something I hadn't told them earlier.

"Hmmmmm," Turner said when I had finished the sad chronicle of recent events. He probed around, asking a dozen or more questions about my time at 25 the Holtons and my finding Gurbeep Singh at Blackwell's casino.

"That was really a stroke of luck, wasn't it, Mr. Polo?"

"That's why people go to casinos," I said. "To get lucky."

"True, true. Then you left Blackwell's with Miss Howard, didn't you?" He went back to his desk drawer and pulled out another photograph. It was Marta Howard, her hair a little longer, a little darker.

"Attractive girl. You went to a nightclub, didn't you?"

"Yes."

"Remember the name?"

"No."

"Could it have been the Helot Club?" Turner asked innocently.

"The what?" I asked, stalling for time, wondering how much Turner already knew about what had happened that night.

"Helot Club."

I shook my head slowly. "Never heard the name before today." At least that much was true.

"It's a private club. Members only. Specializes in introducing its members to"—he paused for dramatic effect—"people who are into some of the more, shall we say, kinky, aspects of adult entertainment. Sometimes the participants are young, quite young."

"I didn't stay long. Loud rock music. Sweaty, bare-chested bartenders. Too crowded for me."

105

Turner slowly eased back into his chair, crossed his legs, and looked at me, waiting for the penny to drop. I imitated him, leaning back in my chair, crossing my legs, and staring at him. At times like this, silence is golden. Your own silence, that is. Outside of the "good-guy, bad-guy" routine, it's the oldest form of witness-interrogation. Lead your victim into an area of doubt, an area where you know he's going to be unsure of himself, then just clam up. Let him sweat. It works most of the time. This wasn't one of those times.

Turner finally broke the silence. "I'm interested in just how you found out about 25 the Holtons. You told Chief Inspector Mandel something about a database check. Can you elaborate on that, please?"

"Sure. I had learned from a local private investigator that the ownership of the shop, BeeJay's, was under the name Carlisle, Inc. I had someone in the States check out Carlisle. Apparently the company had once used the Holtons address."

Turner took the gold pen from its holder and ran it through his fingers like a miniature pool cue. "That's interesting, very interesting. Exactly what database did you use, sir?"

I gave him the name of a large information-processing firm in Southern California that specializes in background checks on businesses.

"Very interesting indeed," Turner replied, managing a small smile. "What else did you learn about Carlisle, Inc.?"

"Nothing. Just that address."

"And the name, sir? Was Gurbeep Singh's name shown?"

"Yes."

"Any other names?"

"Trent. Oliver Trent."

"Ah, yes." Turner slipped the pen back into its holder and beamed at me as if I were a star pupil who had answered a very difficult question. "Oliver Trent. When you met with Gurbeep Singh, at the casino, did you mention Mr. Trent's name?"

"No. There didn't seem to be any reason to bring it up. I simply gave him the envelope I'd been asked to deliver. We didn't have much of a conversation."

106

"And you informed your client, Raymond Singh, that you had accomplished your task?"

"Yes, that's right."

"And what did you client say?"

" 'Good job,' something like that."

"Have you spoken to Raymond Singh since that time?"

"No."

Turner bobbed his head in Carter's direction. "The Chief Inspector had no luck in making telephone contact with Mr. Raymond Singh. We had someone from your immigration department go to see him. He wasn't there. No one at his place of business knew where he was."

"He didn't tell me what his plans were," I said.

Turner said, "There were two young children at 25 the Holtons when you were there. Correct?"

"Yes. I told Carter and Mandel about them."

Turner pressed on. "And when you visited the premises again, with Chief Inspector Carter and Inspector Mandel, you saw evidence of those children, didn't you? Crayoned walls, comics mixed in with pornography. Not a pretty picture, was it?"

"No," I agreed. "Not pretty at all."

"Tell me, then," Turner said, his palms now pressed together in a prayerlike attitude, "do you think that it's possible that your client, Raymond Singh, sent you over here for the purpose of buying one or more of those children? That you, Mr. Polo, were acting as no more than a well-paid procurer? Or—a word that may be more familiar to you—as a pimp?" He blew air out of his lips as if it were cigarette smoke. "Are you a pimp, Mr. Polo?"

15

.

The next twenty minutes or so were pretty ugly. Clive Turner's air of sophistication and upper-class civility peeled away strip by strip like wallpaper from an old boardinghouse dining room. Carter and Mandel took off their gloves and wadded in, throwing accusations the way a heavyweight champ throws jabs. "Pimp" was one of the kinder words directed at me.

My passport lay there on Turner's desk, never out of my sight or out of my mind as I answered their questions and made my own threats, including the usual one about contacting the American Embassy immediately, which didn't impress them very much.

What I learned from their questions was that Gurbeep Singh was suspected of being in the slave trade, that Hardev Singh was in it with him, and that Marta Howard, in addition to operating the Helot Club, was in it with the Singh boys right up to her batting eyelashes. Turner kept hammering away at the connection between Gurbeep and Raymond Singh. While not going so far to risk my life or freedom for Raymond, I couldn't see it.

"Why the hell would Raymond go through this whole elab-

109

orate setup?" I yelled at Turner. "Getting me to come all the way over here, the cashier's check, the tape recording. If they were doing business together, there'd be a simpler way."

"Perhaps," Turner agreed smugly. "Except that we have only your word for the details of the transaction. For all I know, you conduct business on Raymond Singh's behalf all the time, you meet with Gurbeep Singh here on a regular basis."

"You've seen my passport."

Turner picked the passport up and riffled through the pages. "Please," he said in a bored voice. "People engaged in illegal activities seldom use their own passports, Mr. Polo. Surely your exotic career as a police officer taught you at least that much."

We butted heads for another half-hour before Turner finally stood up, hands on hips, arching his back, head pointed toward the ceiling. "You're free to go," he said, in the tone that professional football coaches use to tell fourth-string quarterbacks that it's time to look for another line of work.

"How free?" I said, pointing to my passport.

"Take it," Turner said. "I've already spoken to your Immigration and Naturalization Service. You'll be hearing from them."

The first flight available was not until one in the afternoon. I was at Heathrow by ten, nervously pacing around, expecting Carter or Mandel to show up with leg irons at any moment. I kept trying to call Raymond Singh in San Francisco. All I got connected to was either the sweet young voice that had answered my earlier calls or someone who could barely speak English. The answer was the same either way. Raymond was not there.

I dozed off and on during the flight, thinking about Raymond Singh. Could he be involved in something as disgusting as the slave trade? The sweet young voice that answered his phone could belong to the girl I'd seen at his store, the one who had taken over the cash-register chores, the one with the Levi's so tight Raymond claimed he could see whether a coin in her pocket was heads or tails, the one who was about the same age as Jasmine. What was it that Raymond had said about her? Something to the effect that she was his niece and had been in the country for only a year.

110

The first-class food was wasted on me this trip. I com-
miserated with Dr. Jack Daniels more than I should have, before
falling into a deep, dreamless sleep.

The windows were smeared, the seats filthy, the ashtray
overflowing with long-dead butts, and the taxi driver didn't
know where he was going. I was home at last. I directed him to
Raymond Singh's store first. It was closed. A bad sign. Singh's
mom-and-pop stores kept Las Vegas casino hours.

After several wrong turns and curses about "these fucking
San Francisco hills," the driver deposited me in front of my flat,
watching with watery eyes as I dragged my luggage out of the
back, then sneering when I handed him the exact change for the
excursion. "What about a tip?" It was a demand, not a question.

"Don't play the horses," I told him. His reply was
predictable.

The combination of jet lag and sour-mash whiskey hit me all
at once. I dragged my luggage up the outside steps leading to my
front door. I was halfway up the stairs when the Venetian blinds
in Mrs. Damonte's flat fluttered. She opened her door a crack,
just in case burglars or rapists were trailing behind me. Lucky for
them, they weren't.

If you haven't met Mrs. D. before, you're in for a treat.
She's an octogenarian who was living in her flat before I was
born. When my parents died and left the property to me, Mrs.
D. made her plans: either marry me off to one of her oft-visiting
cousins from the old country or outlive me and take possession
once I was underground. Those odds got better and better for
her every day.

"You're back," she said in Italian.

"Yes. Any problems while I was gone?"

"Nopa," she replied, with one of the very few words of
fractured English she uses occasionally.

I opened a suitcase and handed her one of the Harrods
boxes. The web of wrinkles around her eyes crinkled. "For me?"

"For you, Mrs. Damonte. It's nice to be back."

I staggered up the rest of the steps, hoping I had given her
the right box. Hers held a fine black knit shawl, perfect for wakes

111

and funerals. A day without a wake is like a day without sunshine for Mrs. D. The other box, destined for the lovely hands of Jane Tobin, also contained something black, but it was a little too lacy and brief for Mrs. D., and definitely not meant to be worn at houses of mourning. I dropped the luggage in the living room, trudged into the bedroom, sat on the edge of the bed, kicked my shoes off, and collapsed spread-eagle on the mattress.

It was the smell that woke me up. Mrs. Damonte had sneaked in and left something for me in the kitchen: a big dish of *strangolapreti,* "priest-stranglers," rich little mounds of semolina flour covered with a homemade tomato sauce and grated Parmesan cheese. The legend behind the name was that the dish had been served when priests came to call, and the priests, barely subsisting on the Church's lean and mean diet, would gulp down the food so fast that they'd choke themselves.

I put the dish in the microwave oven and got a pot of coffee going. The kitchen clock showed that it was a little after nine o'clock. If I hadn't been able to see through the window that it was pitch-dark outside, I wouldn't have known whether it was morning or night. I'd left London at one in the afternoon. With an eight-hour time difference, that made it actually five in the morning in San Francisco. The flight had landed at three-thirty, and I'd been home a little after four, which meant that I'd gotten had about a five-hour nap. The microwave timer dinged as I was yawning and debating whether or not to go back to bed.

Mrs. D.'s priest-stranglers brought me close to feeling human again. I refilled the coffee cup and made the thirty-second commute into my office, located in the room adjacent to the kitchen. The mail was neatly stacked alongside the computer. Mrs. D. again. So thoughtful, so helpful, so conscious of the fact that she was paying about nine hundred dollars a month less than what I could rent her flat for. The mail was the usual jumble of junk: bills, a few checks, and a new assignment from an insurance carrier.

I turned on the computer and went to work, starting with Raymond Singh. A statewide assessor check showed that Raymond was doing well indeed. In addition to numerous units in San Francisco, he had property in Marin County, a home in

112

Hillsborough, just down the road, in San Mateo County and one small piece of farmland in Yuba City. I consulted the auto-club tour guide, which gave a brief description of Yuba City: population fourteen thousand; situated in the heart of the largest peach-growing and canning region in the world. Hardly sounded like a place where they auctioned off slaves.

I punched in Gurbeep Singh's name. Nothing came up. I then went through the names from my money guru of persons authorized to sign checks for Carlisle, Inc.: Deepak Yadav, Gurdawer Mand, Jasbir Bhatt, and Jagdeep Sidhu. All I got for my efforts was the notation on the bottom of the screen that I was being charged for eleven minutes of computer line-time. I then tried Oliver Trent. Too much of a good thing. Forty-nine different properties from San Diego to Crescent City under that name, with various middle initials. None in Yuba City.

I drained the last of the coffee and stared at the computer screen, switched to another database, and entered all of those names again for a variety of checks: lawsuits, bankruptcies, small claims, state and federal tax liens, all dusty civil stuff that quite often turns up some interesting information. The information wasn't on line, as they say in computerese, so I'd have to wait until the morning for the results. For checks of driver's licenses, criminal records, and some additional financial information I would also have to wait until tomorrow morning.

I called Raymond's store. No answer. His Hillsborough number was listed in the San Mateo County phone directory. His wife, Arlene, answered the phone. Though I had met Mrs. Singh several times, I doubted that she'd remember me. "I'm working on something important for Raymond, Mrs. Singh. Is he home?"

"Raymond has not been home for some time, I'm afraid. We are separated," she told me. "Everyone knows that," she added. Poor Polo. Always the last to know.

I showered, shaved, and changed into some fresh clothes. It felt good to be wearing something besides gray slacks and a blue blazer. The Burberry would fit in just fine with the San Francisco evening air. I finished off my wardrobe accessories with a .32 Smith and Wesson revolver, holstered at the hip. Well fed, well dressed, well armed, and feeling slightly like Bond getting ready to meet Ernst Starvo Blofeld in some secret cave, I went down to the basement and cranked up the car's engine. The car completely blew the Bond image: a battered, three-year-old Ford with a whip antenna, blackwall tires, and a spotlight. Not exactly an Aston Martin with machine-gun bumpers and revolving license plates, but it makes up for its deficiencies by doing a perfect imitation of an unmarked police car and thus collects very few parking tickets when left in red zones and in front of fire hydrants.

I drove to Raymond Singh's store. It was still closed, though I could see a light coming from the rear, by Raymond's office. The store itself was scrunched under the weight of an eight-story apartment building. I checked the mailbox nameplates. No Singhs were listed. The manager's name was shown just as "Red," in unit number one. I leaned on his doorbell for a long time before hearing the buzzer that released the front door.

Buildings like this made me sad. The lobby must have been rather majestic in its time: marble flooring, thick wood paneling, a lofty ceiling festooned with plaster castings of nymphs being chased by fat little guys with bows and arrows. A staircase at least eight feet wide led up to the mezzanine floor. Now the marble was scratched and stained, the paneling was black with grime, the ceiling was spider-webbed with cracks and the figures that some master plasterer had created were chipped, the gold-filigree painting barely visible.

A bald old guy leaned over the mezzanine railing. "Whaddaya want?" he mumbled.

"Are you Red?" I asked.

One of his hands went to his bald head, smoothing back nothing but scalp. "Ya, whaddaya want?" he repeated.

I fished out my police badge and waved it at him. He leaned so far over the railing I was afraid he'd fall on top of me. I started up the stairs. "Police. I'm wondering what happened to the store next door. It's usually open at this time."

He was wearing a striped pajama top over faded chinos. His bare feet were the color of vanilla ice cream. His hand went to his head again, sliding over his freckled dome. There must have

114

been a pile of red hair there at one time. Now there were just wisps of gray over his ears. "Yeah. I don't know what happened. Been closed last couple of days." He squinted at me through milky eyes. "Damn camel jockeys, you never know about them. Charges a fortune for his shit. I don't shop there, 'less I have to. Get the same stuff for about half-price at Safeway."

"You know the man who owns the store, Ray Singh?"

"Yeah, yeah," he said smacking his lips, then smiling to show me a mouth full of nothing but gums. "Ragheads, you know. Can't trust them."

"When's the last time the store was open?"

He smacked his lips again, and I backed up to get away from the spray. "Day or so. Don't pay much notice, like I said. I do my shopping at Safeway."

"There's a young girl who works there sometimes. Have you seen her?"

Red gave me a view of his gums again. "Little one with the nice tits? Only reason I go in there. Buy a candy bar or something just to look at those tits. Nope. Ain't seen her, either. Why? There some kind of a problem?"

"Could be. How do I get to your back alley?"

"That door there," he said, pointing a trembling finger toward the lobby. "Ain't locked. How come you want to go out there?"

"Just to check the back of the store. You can go back to your apartment. I'll let myself out." He padded away, mumbling something about "damn cops."

The door led out to a small alleyway populated by a row of garbage cans. I regretted not taking a deep breath of the stale lobby air before venturing outside. My shoes made sticky, squishy sounds as I moved cautiously through the debris and around to the back of the lot.

The rear of Singh's store had a heavy metal door protecting it. A stack of flattened cardboard boxes some three feet high butted up against the wall, under a wire-grated window. The cardboard was damp from the fog, and my feet slid back and forth, as if on the deck of a ship, as I strained my eyes peering into the window. A bare light bulb dangled on a cord from the ceiling, illuminating nothing but boxes of canned food and paper goods.

I thought I could hear something. I pressed my ear to the glass. Voices, then music. A radio or TV, left on by mistake? I tapped on the window with my car keys. A small, dark figure crept into the outer limits of the pool of light from the ceiling fixture. I kept tapping away with my keys.

"Go away or I call the police," a nervous young voice shouted.

I brought out my badge and held it close to the window. "I *am* the police. Open up."

16

.

The girl inched forward, shuffling slowly, staying in the dark, avoiding the light as if it might burn her.

I kept waving my badge and repeating, "Police. Open the door."

She finally got near the window. I could see her face, her long, dark hair, and her slim figure. It was the girl Raymond had described as his niece. He had mentioned her name, but I couldn't remember what it was. "Open the door. I'm a friend of Raymond's," I told her.

She moved out of sight. I could hear the metallic scraping of bolts being opened, locks being undone. The door opened with a low screech. She stood there with her arms folded across her chest, shoulders hunched, shaking as if she'd just come out of a freezer. "Are you okay?" I asked. "Remember me? I'm a friend of Raymond. I was in the store a few days ago. At the counter. You came out to the counter, and then Raymond and I went back to his office."

"I—I don't remember," she stammered. Her dark, doelike eyes were wide with fear. "Is Raymond all right?"

"That's what I'm trying to find out." I closed the door and she backed away into the shadows.

"When did you last see him?" I asked, moving so that I was directly under the light fixture.

"He went away. I'm waiting for him to call."

"I was doing a job for Raymond, in London. I called from there. I think I talked to you. Remember? Nick Polo. Did Raymond mention my name?"

Her body language showed that I was getting through to her at last. Her spine stiffened, her arms dropped to her sides. "Oh, yes. Polo. You were really in London?"

"Yes. Listen, Raymond told me your name, but I forgot it."

"Regina," she said.

"Regina. Pretty name for a pretty girl. Where is Raymond?"

She shook her head, sending that smooth black hair swirling around her head. "I don't know. He said he'd call. You want coffee or something?"

"Yes, that sounds good."

I followed her toward the front of the store. She turned right down a narrow hallway just before reaching the office. It was a small room with a single bed against one wall, an office-sized refrigerator stacked on top of one of those combination washer-dryers that do about two pounds of clothes at a time; an unpainted plywood wardrobe closet, the front nothing but a yellow shower curtain on a brass runner; a pine dresser, the top littered with bottles of prescription medicines, cosmetics, after-shave lotion, a bottle of Hennessy cognac; and a TV set with one of those flat, square screens, the picture tube looking even bigger because of the skimpiness of the black plastic cabinet.

Several young, shaven-headed musicians were jumping up and down, hand-syncing away at their electric guitars, while three girls in white spray-on leotards did some steps that looked as if they'd been choreographed by the Marquis de Sade. I silently blessed Regina for having turned the volume off when she'd come to investigate my tapping at the back window. The bed was rumpled, the spread covered with a motley collection of food wrappers: chips, candy bars, those dreadful soup-in-a-cup things.

A Mr. Coffee machine sat on a small stand alongside the bed. The glass decanter was about a third full, and from the smell, the coffee must have been brewed hours earlier. An open package of little chocolate-covered doughnuts about the size of a silver dollar sat next to the coffee machine. I didn't know they still made those little doughnuts and wondered if Raymond's customers dunked them in the contents of those mickey-sized bottles of booze he liked to sell.

"I'll pass on the coffee," I said as the girl was reaching for the pot. I took a better look at her. She was wearing tight jeans again and another cotton T-shirt, this one advertising Diet Pepsi. Old Red next door would have approved. Her hard little nipples were going to wear holes in the cotton in no time. Goose bumps were visible on her golden-brown arms.

"Why don't you put something on, Regina? You look cold."

"No, I'm fine," she said, flopping on the bed, pulling her legs up, and crossing them yoga-style.

"When did you last hear from Raymond?" I asked.

She knitted her brow, sending waves of wrinkles across all that smooth skin. "Two, three days now."

"Where was he going?"

"Raymond never says. Just that—"

"That what?" I urged.

"You really a policeman?"

"No. I used to be. I showed you the badge so you wouldn't be afraid."

She bit down on her lower lip for a moment, then said: "Raymond just said it was business. Family business." Her eyes turned wary. "You know what I mean."

I walked over to her. "No, Regina. I don't know what you mean."

She raised a bent arm over her head as if afraid I was going to hit her. "Raymond said you were helping. You went to London to help."

"Yes, I did. That's why I'm here. I want to help Raymond and you. Tell me, is this where you live?"

"Here?" she laughed. "Oh, no. This is Raymond's. He stays here sometimes, or takes naps during the day."

I walked over to the closet and eased back the curtain.

119

Men's clothes: shirts, jackets, pants. "Where do you live?" I asked her.

"On Hyde Street. I have an apartment there with my mother."

I looked at my watch. "Isn't your mother worried about you?"

She pulled her head in like a turtle's and narrowed her eyes. "No. She's worried about Raymond. You said you were a policeman once. What kind of policeman?"

"Here in San Francisco. That's where I met Raymond. He was accused of a crime. I proved that he didn't do it," I said, hoping the story would loosen her up a bit, get her on my side. She was scared as hell.

I handed her one of my business cards. "You can call me at that number any time, night or day, Regina."

"I hope you can find Raymond now."

"Me too." I settled myself gingerly onto the edge of the bed. "Who did Raymond leave to run the store? Just you?"

She made a face as if she'd bitten into a lemon. "No, Mohinder. He got drunk. He wants to make sex with me. When he left I locked the door. Mohinder doesn't have a key."

"Mohinder?"

"Yes," she said calmly. "He's one of Raymond's cousins."

"Another one of Raymond's cousins? And you're Raymond's niece. Is that right?"

She reached for a bag of barbecue potato chips. "Ummm hmmmm," she said, digging into the chips.

"Regina," I said in a serious tone, "does Raymond like to make love to you?"

"Raymond?" she said, the word distorted by the chips. "No, no, no. He helps me."

"Did he help you get into America?"

She wadded up the bag and threw it toward the TV, undid her legs, and jumped off the bed all in one athletic maneuver, striding to the door. "You are still policeman."

"No. I'm a private detective. I'm helping Raymond."

She stopped at the door, one hand on her hip, the other gripping the doorjamb. I could see she was getting ready to run.

"Listen, Regina. I'm trying to help Raymond. But you have to help me find him. He sent me to London to meet with Gurbeep Singh. Do you know him?"

"No," she said, still looking as if she would bolt at any moment.

"How about a man called Hardev? He's kind of bald and—"

She hissed the name. "Hardev! He make sex with me. Force me on the boat." She started to ramble on in her native tongue. I didn't need a translator to get her impression of Hardev Singh, the man with the butterfly knife at the house in London.

"Look, Regina—" I said, getting to my feet.

She darted out of the room. I could hear the door slamming shut. I went to the back of the store and peeked out into the alleyway. No sign of the girl. I tried Raymond's office, helping myself to one of his Cuban cigars and a hefty slug of cognac while I went through the rubbish on his desk. There were bills, both old and new, dozens of checks from tenants, notes on scratch paper with indecipherable messages.

I switched on the computer and after several frustrating minutes switched it off. I don't know what type of software Raymond used, but it was nothing that I was familiar with. I poked around his desk drawers and file cabinets for a half-hour or so, finding nothing of interest, nothing with the name Gurbeep Singh or Hardev or Oliver Trent or any of those other exotic names I'd come across. I palmed another cigar, then went out the back door and closed it behind me, first worrying about leaving it unlocked, then wondering whether Regina was hiding somewhere behind a garbage can, waiting for me to leave so that she could get back to the little room with the big television set.

17

.

"Don't you guys ever think of buying us something like a cardigan sweater or a jacket?" Jane Tobin asked rather impolitely, removing the midnight-black peignoir from the Harrods box.

She held the lacy garment out in front of her, examining it closely. "Oh, well," she sighed, "at least it isn't a garter-belt ensemble like Roy—oops."

She wasn't fooling me. Years of investigative training had me deducing that Roy's last name wasn't really "Oops." The only Roy who came to my mind was Rogers, and I had the feeling that old Roy wasn't the cad who had presented Jane with that most sexy of undergarments. The last time I'd seen Roy, he looked as if he was past the age of pulling the trigger, so to speak.

"Just what is a garter-belt ensemble?" I asked innocently.

"It really is pretty, Nicky," she said, choosing to ignore my question. "Beautiful lace." She folded the peignoir neatly back into its box, then tiptoed over and planted a kiss on my lips.

Jane is a reporter/columnist for the *San Francisco Bulletin*. The slash in the middle of her job description came about due to a recent cutback in employees at the newspaper, so now, in

123

addition to her three-times-a-week column, written on whatever strikes her fancy, as long as the editor agrees, she is also handling some general news stories.

Jane pulled back, ran a hand through her wedge-cut auburn hair, put a finger to my lips, and blew on it, her way of telling me that Roy and the garter belt were a dead issue. We had been seeing each other for a couple of years now on a fairly regular basis, but always with the option of seeing others when we felt the need. Jane had suffered through a rough marriage and a rougher divorce and was not looking for any permanent involvements at the moment.

"Let me fix you a drink," she said. "Then you can tell me all about London."

So I did, bringing her right up to date with my visit to Raymond Singh's store the night before.

Jane poured us both another glass of Chardonnay. We were at her apartment, before going out to lunch.

"Nice wine, isn't it?" she asked.

"Terrific," I agreed.

"I'm doing a story on the smaller wineries in the Napa Valley."

"So they supplied you with some freebies," I said, taking another sip of the chilled wine. It's one of the reasons reporters and cops get along so well. Both professions live by the same creed: if you have to pay for it, it's not worth it, "it" being food, booze, or tickets to a theatrical or sporting event.

"I met Raymond Singh once. During the last presidential campaign. He was a heavy contributor. Seemed like an all-right guy."

"I thought so, too, or I never would have taken the job."

Jane's malachite-green eyes twinkled a bit. "Yes, I imagine it was a real hard sell to get you to London. You did say the Ritz, didn't you?"

"Nice thing about the Ritz is that it's within walking distance of Harrods."

Her face turned serious. "What do you think, Nick? Is Raymond involved in some kind of"—she rolled her hand around, causing her gold bracelets to make clinking noises as she searched for the right words—"slave trading?"

"His cousin Gurbeep sure is. And the guy with the knife, Hardev, definitely is. The house in London was loaded with porno crap. I'm pretty sure that the videotape the London cop played was of Jasmine, the girl at the nightclub."

"And the children at the house, just babies." Her shoulders shuddered. "God, the stories you hear. Makes you sick. They say there's a big market out there for children. Any race, any age. Delivered anywhere for a price. A lot of it involves people who'll do anything to adopt an infant, but too much of it is just sex creeps."

"I wouldn't trust Raymond in a card game and I might not buy a used car from him. But selling kids? No, I don't buy it. If he is, though, I'm going to find him and turn him over to the police."

"What about the girl at the store? What was her name?"

"Regina."

"Doesn't sound East Indian."

I nodded. "Raymond said something about her being here a short time and acting like an American already. She probably picked a new name." I sipped the wine, then said: "She was scared, Jane, really scared, last night. I almost had her trusting me, but she kept going back to my being a policeman. She's scared to death of the cops."

"You think she's an illegal, then."

"It's a good bet. If so, Raymond brought her into the country, or at least paid to have it done."

"And he's using her?"

"Not for sex. At least that's what she says. Hardev Singh, he's the one she said 'make sex with me.' On a boat. Probably some old freighter they used to transport her over here."

"So what now?"

"Find Raymond. I could use some help. I'd like you to run his name and some others through the paper's library."

"Ah," she said, reaching over and fingering the lacy peignoir. "There was a motive behind this lavish gift."

"Just seeing you wearing it would be motive enough."

125

She smiled and settled her half-filled wineglass on the coffee table. "You *have* been gone a long time, and I *have* missed you."

"Are you trying to make sex with me?" I asked in a shocked tone.

She leaned toward me. "If you play your cards right, I might even wear Roy's garter belt."

18

.

All the civil-court data checks I ordered took over an hour to sift through, and I came up with nothing. Raymond Singh was involved in dozens of civil suits, includiing the divorce from his wife. The rest of the names came back as complete zeros.

The easiest thing to do would be to sit back and wait a few days, then run a credit-card check on Raymond. But it takes Visa, MasterCard, and American Express a few weeks to post the latest charges on their billing forms, the forms my computer wizard was able to access. And if Raymond was playing around with illegal aliens, he might not be using credit cards, at least those under his own name.

All of which left me with one alternative: the phone company. My source at one of Ma Bell's problem children was sorry to tell me that it would take a full day to get the information I needed: all toll calls from the numbers at Raymond's office. Since he had four separate lines, I was going to have to check them all. Obtaining telephone records on someone other than yourself is, of course, illegal. It is also expensive, but I planned to bill Raymond Singh for the records, if he turned up alive and wasn't involved in the selling of human beings. If it turned out he was involved, I'd gladly write off the expenses and do everything I could to put him in jail, or, as my cellmates at the federal prison in Lompoc preferred to call their temporary government abode, the Crossbar Hotel.

I spent the night trying to rid myself of jet lag, get back on balance, and induce Jane Tobin to model that black peignoir. She bounced out of her bed bright and early, ready for work the next morning, while I dragged around with barely enough energy to make it back to my flat and fall back into bed again.

I called Inspector Paul Paulsen, my former partner, now attached to the General Works Detail at the Hall of Justice, and gave him Raymond's name, along with Oliver Trent, Gurbeep ("Gordy") Singh, and the rest of those exotic East Indian names, to run through Department of Motor Vehicles and criminal records.

Here again I was not only bending the law but breaking it cleanly. Criminal records are not generally withheld from public scrutiny. You can go to your local county clerk and check a name through the files. The problem is that if you are not sure just where the subject committed the crime, you'd have to check at every county courthouse in the country to find out what was available. The law-enforcement computer database takes away all that hassle by making it possible to check with California Investigation and Identification, the National Criminal Information Center, and finally the reliable old FBI.

Department of Motor Vehicles records can be reviewed by a licensed private investigator, if he is bonded and the request for the information complies with state standards, such as searching for a witness to an accident in order to serve a subpoena on him. To get a hit on your request you need the driver's license number or the subject's date of birth. Of course, the law-enforcement computers work around all those nagging details.

Unfortunately, all of my requests came up negative or unconfirmed, since I didn't have a date of birth, a Social Security number, or any positive ID, except, of course, for Raymond Singh, who had not been arrested since that homicide charge I had investigated long ago. The DMV listed his addresses as the store in the tenderloin and his house down on the peninsula.

Oliver Trents were numerous in the DMV files, but there were none in the Bay Area, or in or near Yuba City.

I spent most of the day catching up on paperwork and taking another nap. At a few minutes after five I was waiting at the bar of the Fly Trap restaurant at Second and Folsom streets, just up the block from one of Pacific Bell's major office buildings.

My phone source, a tall, thin gentleman in his thirties, with clear blue eyes and a shock of blond hair that flopped boyishly over his forehead, came in and looked around the bar cautiously before coming over to me. He ordered a Corona light, then slid a thick white envelope to me in a manner that suggested he had been watching too many spy movies and was worried that the phone company's version of the KGB would rush up at any moment and slap handcuffs on both of us.

I followed his routine and dropped a plain white envelope filled with the necessary twenty-dollar bills into his coat pocket. We chatted about baseball and the weather long enough for him to order another beer. Then he filled me in with the latest phone-company jargon.

"Can't get LUDs, Nick. I assume you knew that."

"LUDs," I said, trying to phrase my response so that he wasn't sure whether I knew or not.

"Local Usage Dialing. I mean, I saw a cop show on TV the other night. A cop goes to the phone company and gets LUDs on some guy. Can you imagine that?"

"Unbelievable, I guess."

"Guess? You know it. Have any idea how many computers it would take just to store local calls? I mean when you get your phone bill, all you see is the monthly charge, then the toll calls, right?"

"Absolutely." I was begging to sound like Major Pickering responding to Henry Higgins in *My Fair Lady*.

"Of course, MUDs are even more confusing."

"MUDs."

He raised an eyebrow and studied me for a moment. "Measured Usage Dialing. You know, the FCNS, Frequently Called Numbers, that you can have set up to be billed at a lower rate, like if you're calling someone all the time in another toll area. Now, if the cops went to get those, it'd be okay. Those or toll calls. You'd think they'd check on this crap before they make the damn show."

"Sloppy of them," I agreed.

There were a few more minutes of this, in which I learned that he was now working out of CNA—Central Names and Addresses—and was hoping to be moved to DPAC, which had something to do with dedicated offices that assigned new numbers to company service reps and linemen who were installing or repairing phones. My head full of possibly useful knowledge that I would no doubt forget in a matter of minutes, I bought him a final drink, then walked back to my car and started checking the list of Raymond Singh's latest phone calls.

Raymond had been a busy boy. There were dozens of toll calls. My source had dutifully scribbled the listed names and addresses alongside the numbers. Most were for business firms that had no visible connection to what I was looking for. There was one call to the Burlingame Travel Bureau, the same agency Raymond had used to book my London trip. I should have thought of that angle myself. If Raymond was traveling, he'd probably have used the same travel agent.

And there were three calls to a Sidhu, 1462 Stone Road, Yuba City. No notation as to whether Sidhu was a first or a last name. Yuba City. My money man had told me that Gurbeep Singh's accounts showed a lot of activity in Bombay, Calcutta, London, Vancouver, San Francisco, and Yuba City. The Stone Road address was certainly worth checking out.

After years of wondering what it was my feet were sticking to in public phone booths, I had finally broken down and got a car phone, though I used it reluctantly and only for calls I didn't care were overheard, because as we all know now, listening in on CMTs—cellular mobile telephones—is as easy as turning on the television and in fact is done by a lot of people who are bored with what's on TV—imagine how many of us there are—and get a kick out of being audio peeping Toms.

Burlingame is one of the nicer peninsula bedroom communities, located just a few miles south of the international airport.

I had picked up my travel tickets in person from the owner of Burlingame Travel, Gloria Perret, a very attractive, very sharp lady who remembered my name right away.

"Nice to hear from you, Mr. Polo," Ms. Perret said, her voice coming across in that slightly garbled, breathless way they do on cellular phones. "How was London?"

"Terrific, thanks. I'm trying to get a hold of Raymond Singh, Gloria. He told me he was going on a trip, but I forgot where he told me he would be staying."

"Hold the line. I'll get the information for you," she said.

I put the car in motion and pointed it toward North Beach while I waited.

"Here it is, Mr. Polo. The Pacific Hotel, Vancouver, British Columbia."

"Did Raymond say when he was coming back?" I said, swerving out of the way and just missing a pickup truck whose driver must have flunked the license-examination question relating to the purpose of red lights.

"No."

"What about the return flight?"

"None," Perret said. "Just first class one way to Vancouver two days ago. Raymond said something about flying back with someone who had a private jet."

I thanked her for the information. Private jet. My, my. The information operator supplied me with the number for the Pacific Hotel in Vancouver, and the desk clerk told me that Mr. Raymond Singh had never checked into the hotel.

I met Jane for dinner at the Stinking Rose, on Columbus Street, just a few blocks from my flat. The restaurant was named after the garlic bulb, a condiment it used to delicious excess in all of its entrées. Jane had a raft of computer paper from the *Bulletin*'s library. She'd struck out on all the names, with the exception of Raymond Singh. The stories on Raymond were mostly about political fund-raising and some of those lawsuits he was involved in.

"You told me there was a Yuba City connection," she said, finishing up the last of her fettuccini, "so I ran the town name and cross-referenced immigrants and illegal aliens." She handed me a sheaf of the dot-matrix computer paper, which when unfolded reached a good eight feet in length.

The lead story concerned an article on the Rand McNally map-publishing company, which had apparently had the temerity to list Yuba City as the least desirable habitat in the United States. The citizens of Yuba City strongly disagreed, especially the members of the World Sikh Organization, who pointed out that between a million and a million and a half East Indians had left the Punjab to settle in the United States, Britain, and Canada.

A great many had settled in the Sacramento Valley. One person was quoted as calling Yuba City the New Delhi of the Western world, pointing out that many immigrants worked in the peach, walnut, and almond orchards in the farming area around Yuba City. All of which meant not much to me, except that if you were smuggling East Indians into the United States, Yuba City was certainly a good point to drop them off and let them assimilate into American culture before moving them on.

There were several other stories on Yuba City. It and its neighboring sister city, Marysville, were abundant in wildlife, especially beaver. The famous mountain man Jedediah S. Smith had been the first white man to set foot there, much to the regret of the Yuba Maidu Indians. Both cities thrived as centers of trade for the gold mines in nearby Nevada, Butte, and Placer counties.

"Well, what do you think?" Jane asked, as a steaming plate of prawns was placed in front of her.

"I think I'm headed for Yuba City."

19.

"There's not enough room for my luggage," Jane complained, looking into my car's trunk the following morning. I had carried three pieces of matched black vinyl bags from her apartment to the carport.

She was right. The trunk was jammed with camera gear, electronic devices, and my lone suitcase. "Don't worry," I told her. "We may not be staying overnight. I have a feeling Yuba City is not the fun capital of Northern California." I stacked her bags in the backseat. "And besides, I don't think you're going to get much out of this trip anyway."

Her eyes squinted like Clint Eastwood's just before he pulls out that long-barreled revolver. There was a story somewhere in all this mess. Her reporter's red corpuscles were bubbling away at a high pitch. "We'll see" was all she said before getting into the car. Clint would have been proud of her.

There are certain "the's" that you have to learn if you spend much time around the Bay Area. San Francisco is "the" city. Lake Tahoe is "the" lake. The Russian River in nearby Sonoma County is "the" river. The Golden Gate Bridge is "the" bridge. To get to Yuba City from "the" city, you have to take the other bridge, the good gray Bay Bridge. The ride from west to east doesn't show you much. You travel along the bottom span, the one that was originally used by streetcars. The railings are high enough to block the views, but to make up for that the bridge authority made this trip free. Coming back the other way costs a buck, but it's worth it. Probably the best view of the San Francisco skyline is from mid-span on the Bay Bridge.

Once off the bridge, you travel in a northeasterly direction, skirting the towns of Emeryville, Berkeley, Richmond, Rodeo, and Crockett before crossing the Carquinez Bridge, a dollar ride that should go for about a nickel. Then you're in Vallejo, a town famous for its whorehouses during the Second World War and not much since.

The heavy rains of March had not done a lot to reduce years of drought, but they had done wonders for the scenery. The lush green hills were rouged with poppies, more of the beautiful orange state flowers than I had seen in years. Waves of wild mustard were everywhere, along with pockets of buttercups, wild radishes, purple irises, and lupines.

Jane had her AAA maps out and was acting as navigator. "I think our best bet is to cut north on Ninety-nine just before we reach Sacramento," she said, head bent over her maps, yellow marking pencil in hand.

"You're the boss," I said.

She looked up and smiled. "I'm glad you agree on that. Let's find someplace for breakfast." We stopped in Fairfield, which, though just some fifty miles from San Francisco, has a flat, midwestern feel about it. The restaurant was crowded with service men and women from nearby Travis Air Force Base.

Back on the road again, Jane began calling off directions that got us off Highway 80 and eventually onto Highway 99, which for no noticeable reason became Highway 70. After a few more miles we came to a fork in the road that put us back on Highway 99. I've always wondered whether the people who gave numbers to freeways did that as just a part-time job, something to do when they weren't developing simplified tax forms for the Internal Revenue Service.

There was a lot of flat farmland, most of it barren, with

single tractors plowing up small dust storms as they dug those chalk-line-straight furrows. We passed numerous trucks pulling double gondolas filled to the top with sugar beets. Every so often there would be a field of shimmering green onions spreading right up to the roadside, so thickly grown together that they barely budged from the zephyrs created by the seventy-plus-mile-an-hour vehicular traffic whizzing by, including those huge sugar-beet carriers. Then we hit the orchards, miles and miles of them. They stretched all the way to Yuba City.

There used to be a time when small towns had their own individual flavor: a slightly different architectural pattern, different specialty stores, different flavors to the food, different looks to the natives. Yuba City looked as if it could have been any other small town, or a section of San Diego, Los Angeles, San Jose, San Francisco, or Sacramento, with its K Mart, J. C. Penney, Taco Bell, Kentucky Fried Chicken, Long's Drugs, and self-service Chevron and Shell stations.

"Where to now?" Jane asked.

"We're looking for Stone Road," I said. "We'd better find a gas station."

We did. I topped up the Ford's tank and checked the oil and tire pressure while Jane chipped in and used the station's dirty squeegee to scrape away the remains of dozens of bugs that had ended their life cycle against the windshield. For a dollar and a half I was allowed to buy a map of Yuba City.

"Map's got Marysville on it, too," said the bored teenager with grease-smeared coveralls sitting inside the thick glass cage. I wondered how he got the coveralls dirty, since he didn't do anything but sit on a stool and accept cash or credit cards. There was a sign just over the metal slot where you pass your money through that proclaimed, "This booth videotaped twenty-four hours a day." "How's it feel to be in show business?" I asked the kid.

"Huh?" he asked, eyes glazed and staring over my shoulder. I turned around and followed his line of vision. Jane was leaning over, working the squeegee, standing on her tiptoes, which stretched her white shorts to their limits.

135

"Too bad that won't be on the video," I said, counting my change and getting nothing but another "Huh?" in response.

Stone Road was a narrow strip of asphalt bordered on both sides by fruit trees, an occasional house showing through the foliage. Number 1462 had a chain-link fence topped by barbed wire fronting it and a filigree iron gate blocking the road leading into the property. A mile or so away, a lone hot-air balloon, with an orange-and-yellow striped pattern, dangled like a Christmas-tree ornament under the clear blue sky.

I got out of the car and walked over to the gate, my feet making crunching sounds on the gravel. A sturdy lock on a chrome chain circled the twin gate doors. I looked for a bell of some type, saw none, and settled for rattling the doors.

"What now?" Jane called from the car.

"Beep the horn. Let's try to wake someone up. I don't want to have to climb this damn fence."

I studied the doors while we waited: an expensive piece of workmanship, each door topping off at more than eight feet. Small spikes, painted in the same flat black as the gates, studded the top of each door. There were two small boxes, the size of a pack of matches, welded to the back side of each door. They served no decorative function. A burglar alarm? I shook the gates as hard as I could.

A battered pickup truck that had come off the assembly line a glossy black but was now a dusty charcoal color, came careening through the fruit trees, skidding to a halt inches from the gates. A short, deep-chested man with dark hair under a cowboy-style straw hat got out from behind the driver's seat. He had a bushy pirate's beard and was wearing faded jeans, a chambray shirt, and buckskin boots that reached almost to his knees. His shirtsleeves were rolled up to his biceps, revealing well-muscled, hairless arms. He carried a double-barreled shotgun in one hand.

"What do you want?" He had a heavy accent, but there was a snap to his voice, like a whip cracking.

"I'm interested in buying some property. Is the owner around?"

"No."

"How about Mr. Sidhu?"

136

Pirate Beard moved the shotgun up slowly, cradling the barrels in the crook of one arm. "Don't know the name."

"He owns a lot of land around here. Saw it listed on the maps in the assessor's office," I said, adding one more little white lie to my repertoire.

"Don't know the name," he repeated firmly.

"You must have a boss. Can I speak to him?"

He lips parted, large white teeth flashing against his dark skin. I couldn't tell whether it was his version of a smile or a snarl. "No." A man of few words.

"Where can I reach him? Vancouver, maybe?"

He pushed off from the pickup truck, coming toward me, his body at an angle, so that the shotgun barrels were protruding through the gate's iron bars, pointed right at me. "Who are you, mister?"

Jane got out of the car, stumbling over toward us, almost losing her footing in the gravel.

"What's wrong?" she asked in a sweet, innocent voice.

His eyes swiveled between us, then settled on my car. I could see his lips move slightly as he read the license plate.

"The man says that Mr. Sidhu isn't here, darling."

"Darn," she said, digging a toe into the gravel. A wonderful little performance. Jane had started her newspaper career as a sports writer, one of the first to invade the sanctity of the locker room. "Darn" was not exactly a locker-room word.

"My wife is really interested in buying some land up here," I said, relieved to see that the shotgun barrels had dropped toward the ground.

"Yes," Jane piped in, her arm encircling my waist. "We need a tax write-off. You know how it is. No write-offs, old Uncle Sam just scoops up everything."

He raked his beard with the fingers of one hand. "I just work here. You're wasting your time." He walked back to the pickup, jerked the door open, and tossed the shotgun onto the front seat. Then he revved the engine, put the gear in reverse, and backed away at high speed, sending pea-sized pieces of gravel shooting off in all directions.

"Not exactly a member of the Chamber of Commerce, was

137

he?" Jane said, waving a hand in front of her face to fend off the small storm of dust created by the departing truck. "What do we do now, Nick?" I was wondering how to respond to that very question when my eyes picked up the balloon again.

20

■

It was one of those huge pickup trucks with monster wheels hoisting the chassis three full feet above the ground, metallic green with chrome dripping all over it. There was a chrome winch attached to the front bumper. Attached to the winch was a thick line of rope traveling skyward to the hot-air balloon.

A girl in her twenties with tousled brown hair was sitting cross-legged alongside the truck. She got to her feet when she saw Jane and me approaching, and brushed off her designer jeans with both hands, keeping a wary eye on us.

"Hi," I said. "I'm Nick. This is Jane."

Our names didn't make much of an impression. She planted her hands on her hips. A pale-yellow tank top showed off her tan. "I'm Donna. What do you want?"

I pointed up toward the balloon. "I was hoping to get a ride. I'll be happy to pay you what you think it's worth."

Donna scoffed. "Ain't worth nothin' to me, mister. I wouldn't go up there for anything with that crazy son of a bitch Lennie."

I tilted my head back. I could make out two dark heads up in the balloon's basket, one male, the other female. "Think there's a chance Lennie will give me a ride?"

139

She shrugged her shoulders. "You can ask him. I sleep with him and eat with him, but I don't go on rides with him."

I leaned back and waved to the balloon. It looked about a couple of hundred feet up. "Can you hear me?" I shouted.

The man's head leaned over the basket, way over the basket. He started making gestures, pointing a finger at me, then turning the finger back to himself, then pantomiming himself on a telephone.

I gave an exaggerated nod of my head and shouted, "Yes!"

The man leaned even further out of the basket, waved both hands in greeting, then suddenly leaped from the basket, hands together, legs bent, like a kid showing off from a swimming-pool diving board. He plunged down right at us. All I could yell was "Run!" I reached for Jane, not really sure which way to go. He kept coming. I could swear I saw a smile on his face. Then suddenly he changed direction, jerking back upward, then bouncing down again, like a yo-yo running out of steam. I heaved a sigh of relief and looked at Jane. Her complexion matched the color of her shorts, hospital white.

Donna laughed loudly. "I told you the son of a bitch was crazy, didn't I?"

After five jerky up-and-down swings, the bungee cord straightened out, and I could see the shoulder and seat harness wrapped around the man's body. He did a graceful turn so that he was upside down, head pointed right at me. "You want to talk to me?" he asked in an amazingly calm voice.

While Donna worked with the balloon's tether line, she told us about her crazy son-of-a-bitch friend. He was into the sport of bungee-diving, but because people with much saner heads than Lennie had put a stop to letting bungee-divers use bridges and freeway overpasses as launching pads, he had recently bought the hot-air balloon.

"Does he know how to fly the damn thing?" Jane asked, having already informed me that she thought that Donna was an extremely intelligent young lady, because she firmly agreed with her about not getting into the balloon's basket. "I'm not going anywhere with that crazy son of a bitch" were her exact words.

Once the balloon was safely settled on the ground, a broad-shouldered man leaped over the basket railing and sauntered over to us. He seemed to be in his forties. His dark hair was combed straight back from a widow's peak. He had a broad grin on his face and looked like a man who went through life with a broad grin on his face.

"Lennie Nordeman," he said, "Hope I didn't scare the shit out of you." He clicked his eyes over to Jane. "Actually, I kind of hope I did scare the shit out of him, but not you, pretty lady." He kept the grin on his face as he spoke. Jane apparently found the grin infectious, and she smiled back at him.

Lennie rubbed his hands together like a man anticipating a gourmet meal, his eyes still on Jane. "What's up? You want to try some bungee-diving with me? You'll love it."

Jane's response finally wiped the grin off his face, but he shrugged good-naturedly. "How about you, fella?"

"The balloon, yes. The dive, no."

Fifteen minutes later I was lofting skyward with Lennie and another beautiful brunette, Annie, who turned out to be Donna's younger sister. "Younger by five years," she pointed out, batting her eyes in Lennie's direction.

"Just how high can we go?" I asked, my hands digging into leather handrails covering the wicker siding of the basket.

"Hell, we could go up a thousand feet, but then I'd have to let go of the tether line. No telling where we'd end up."

My stomach was starting to do little flip-flops as I watched the glimmering auburn top of Jane's head get smaller and smaller below us. The basket was pretty small, about four and a half feet square. With the three of us, a large propane fuel tank, and an ice chest, there wasn't much room to maneuver. The white-vinyl-jacketed bungee cord was coiled snakelike near the ice chest.

"I'm interested in taking a look at that orchard over there," I said, pointing toward the Sidhu property.

"Let's see how it looks when we get up a couple of hundred feet," Lennie said, opening the ice chest and pulling out two long-necked Budweisers. He handed me one of the beer bottles, then said: "Maneuvering these babies is a bitch. I'm still learning. The way it works is, you go with the wind. Say the wind is

141

blowing westerly at a hundred feet. Then you get to a hundred feet and go with the flow. If the wind at two hundred feet is blowing east and you want to go east, then you climb to two hundred feet."

"What if you want to go north or south?" I asked.

He uncapped the beer bottle and took a deep swig. "Got to find at what height the wind is blowing that way. Tricky stuff, huh?"

"Yes," I agreed, spreading my feet out as the balloon began rocking back and forth. The wind was light. The only sounds were the creaking of the wicker basket and the propane steadily blazing away in the burner some eight feet overhead.

We got up to two hundred feet, the end of the tether line. I used a pair of binoculars I'd dug out of the Ford's trunk and scanned the Stone Road property, starting at the entrance gate. The wire-topped fence encircled all of the property that I could see: acres and acres of fruit trees, then in the middle a huge pinkish stucco house with turrets and balconies; several large, hangar-shaped buildings and, like a needle on a compass, a straight line of asphalt carved out of the fruit trees. A runway. Mr. Sidhu had his own private little airfield. I fiddled with the binoculars' zoom-focus ring, finally picking up the bright-silver tail of a business-sized jet plane near one of the hangars. Raymond Singh had told Gloria Perret, the travel agent, that he was flying back from Vancouver on a private jet.

"We can go down now," I told Lennie. "I've seen all I need to."

"Sure, pal," he said amiably, handing me his empty beer bottle, then bending down and reaching for the bungee cord. "I'm gonna try one more dive. Then we'll go down. Annie will keep you company while I'm gone." He strapped on the harness, whistling a happy tune to himself, as Annie stared at him with adoring eyes. Outside of Lennie himself, she was probably the only one around who didn't think he was a crazy son of a bitch.

21.

The county courthouse was a new building of raw concrete and marble floors. A tip to those of you whose travels may take you to and through small towns. No matter what the courthouse looks like, the bathrooms there will be cleaner than those of any of the service stations or restaurants in town. The kings and queens of civil service spare no expense on their thrones.

Jane was as used to digging through court records as I was, so we made quick work of checking on the property and permits at Stone Road. The airfield had gone in three years ago. Construction on that semi-castle I'd seen from the balloon had started at the same time. The assessor's records were confusing, but using their plot map we got what I was sure was a pretty good outline of the property behind the wire fence. It was broken up into numerous parcels, all under the last name Sidhu, but with different first initials: just plain R., then R.A., R.J., J.R., L., L.M., and through the alphabet, all the way down to Z. Sidhu. Put all together, it totaled more than seven hundred acres. I had copies made from the map book and sketched in the areas where the gate, the house, and the airfield should be.

We checked into the Tree Top Motel, which looked as

classy as anything in town, then went out and rented a truck and a ladder and made a purchase at a pet shop. Dinner was at the motel's coffee shop. I followed my father's advice: "When in doubt, order a club sandwich. Not much they can screw up with a club sandwich."

Jane felt adventurous and tried "the catch of the day," which turned out to be soggy filet of snapper in a sauce that tasted like leftover Thanksgiving gravy. She cleverly supplied me with one spoonful of the fish and sauce, after which I ended up putting half of my sandwich onto her plate.

Old habits die hard: opening doors for women, young and old, who either are gratefully surprised or fix you with a "You're patronizing me, you chauvinist bastard" stare; calling waitresses "honey," which gets more of those stares and possibly coffee aimed toward the rim of the cup when you want a refill; and sharing food with your companion when her choice is "the catch of the day."

We lingered over coffee until it got dark. Then I drove the rental truck out to Stone Road, Jane trailing behind in the Ford. I edged the truck, which was of a size about midway between a pickup and one of those furniture-moving vans, up as close as possible to the chain-link fence, about a hundred yards down from the entrance gate, then manhandled the aluminum extension ladder up to the truck's roof, some ten feet above the ground.

Jane watched with arms crossed and a look of amusement on her face. "Is this the way cat burglars really act?" she asked, as I clambered up onto the truck's hood, hoisting myself up to the roof.

"No," I admitted, squeezing my eyes shut at the scraping noise the ladder made as I extended it full length. Full length was twenty-four feet, the man at the tool-rental agency had assured me. I reached down, and Jane handed me the knapsack filled with tools of the trade, some of which I hoped I wouldn't have to use.

I edged the bottom of the ladder up over the fence, making sure I didn't make contact with the barbed wire on top. Even with the leather gloves I was wearing, I wouldn't have wanted to be holding onto a heavy piece of aluminum if the fence was electrified. Whether or not the fence was wired had been a real concern. How much juice would it take to wire a fence of that size? And how much of a jolt would there be?

I carefully guided the ladder over the fence and down to the ground, then nestled the top end gently against the side of the truck. A good five feet of overhang stood up above the truck roof's top. From there all I had to do was swing out and climb down. The angle from ladder to ground wasn't very steep. My weight caused the ladder to buckle but not enough to bring the aluminum in contact with the fence or the barbed wire. Once safely on the ground, I tilted the ladder upright and lowered it by walking backward, grabbing one rung at a time. I dragged the ladder over to the nearest line of trees.

It was a cloudless night. The moon was at about the halfway point. Half-full? Or, since I was feeling slightly pessimistic at the moment, maybe "half-empty" was a better description. Not for the first time in my life, I wished I had joined the Boy Scouts or some useful organization that taught youngsters how to navigate by the stars, rather than occupying myself during an interesting if misspent youth by stealing fruit from grocery stores, playing eightball in poolrooms, and learning poker and card tricks from my uncle Dominic. My other uncle, Sam, had provided some technical courses during boot camp that were supposed to turn me and my fellow draftees into Apachelike warriors. We soon learned that in the real army, what you did was imitate a sled dog and hope that the lead dog knew where he was going.

Jane called out to me, "You okay over there?"

"Yeah. Fine."

"Let's synchronize our watches," she said, sounding like a commander about to send the troops out of the trenches.

"Eight-forty-five," I said, after squinting at my Timex.

"Right," responded Jane. "If you're not back in an hour, I use your car phone to call the cops." She gave me a friendly wave, then said, "Look out for dogs, Nick."

Dogs. The thought of drooling Rottweilers or German shepherds scared me a lot more than electrified fences. In my jacket pocket were three rawhide bones saturated with some-

145

thing that dogs preferred to anything else, according to the pet-shop owner. I hoped anything included my arms and legs.

I took a four-cell black metal Mag-Lite flashlight, the type that cops use as a nightstick—or, using the present politically correct terminology, impact tool—from the knapsack on my back, checked the assessor's map, and started off in what I hoped was the right direction, staying between rows of fruit trees. The ground was mushy, as if it had been irrigated earlier in the day. I kept going for a good ten minutes at a steady pace. The flashlight beam adjusted from a wide angle to a pinpoint. I kept it in a narrow range that illuminated just a circle of three feet or so.

I could see the house coming up. Everything was going smoothly. No sign of dogs, tripwires, or roving guards. There were floodlights spaced around the house and the buildings near the airfield. The closer I got, the more the house looked like something from a movie about Ali Baba and the forty thieves, all curving stucco, with a huge, gold-tipped, onion-shaped dome surrounded by four flanking towers jutting up some fifty feet, a full two or three stories higher than the dome. Neat rows of Italian cypresses ringed the visible portions of the building.

I slowed down, dropped to one knee, and reached into the knapsack for the Tracker's Ear, a fancy, frontierlike name for an electronic sound-amplification device. The advertisements promote them as just terrific for carrying around in the woods and jungle to listen for deer and other game. There may, in fact, be a hunter trekking around with the padded earphones snapped to his head and the hand-held, Ping-Pong-paddle-shaped amplifier in one hand, waiting for Bambi to say something to Thumper, but like many products made for honest, useful purposes, the Tracker's Ear can be put to other uses, such as picking up whispered conversations a hundred yards away.

Luckily, the device has a safety circuit that automatically shuts down when the noise level exceeds a hundred decibels, because I had no sooner turned the damn thing on when all hell broke loose: loud, raucous, ear-splitting screams. Then something huge dropped down from the tree overhead.

I rolled to the ground, swinging the flashlight around my head like a cowboy twirling a lasso. The throaty, screaming

146

sound was like nothing I'd never heard before, and it was all around me. I groped for the .32 revolver holster at my hip. The flashlight's beam finally came to rest on a pair of beady, bright eyes no more than five feet from me. The bobbing head was attached to a big bird. Its beak was opening and closing, and that screeching was sound coming from its long throat. Suddenly the bird's tail opened up, the feathers fanning out, revealing large blue-and-green eyespots: a peacock. I was surrounded by a flock of screaming peacocks.

The birds froze in place when the flashlight beam bathed them in light. I found the Tracker's Ear and started running, trying to keep my balance as my feet slithered on the wet earth. The peacocks were screeching and jumping out of the way, some snapping out with their beaks as I raced by. I had read somewhere that peacocks were used as guard birds, much as geese are, and like geese, they'll attack when frightened.

I broke clear of the orchard of trees, my feet pounding on dry dirt, then finally on a paved road leading to a concrete-block building with a roof of overlapping corrugated sheet metal. I ducked behind a line of oil drums, waited for my breath to come back to somewhere near normal, then took a peek. A pair of headlights were boring holes into the darkness over where I had run into the peacocks.

I hooked up the Tracker's Ear and pointed it in that direction, then dug the binoculars out of the knapsack. The truck looked like the same one I'd seen earlier by the gate. The guy with the bushy pirate beard got out from behind the wheel. His companion was tall and thin, seemed to be in his twenties, and was wearing a matching khaki shirt and pants. I fiddled with the Tracker's Ear, adjusting the volume control up to its highest reading.

I could hear the peacocks screeching and the truck's engine idling. The two men were shining flashlights at the ground and up into the trees. There was some muffled conversation I couldn't make out. Then, as they made their way back to the truck, a sentence came in loud and clear. "Fucking mating season. Bastards drive you nuts." Then the truck's doors slammed shut and the motor revved up.

I took a deep sigh and let out the breath slowly. Saved by Mother Nature's never-ending life cycle. Or, to put it another way, a bunch of horny birds. The truck's headlight beams headed off toward the main house. I waved the sound amplifier around full circle but picked up nothing other than the peacocks.

I heaved myself back to my feet and started exploring. The concrete-block building was nothing more than a shed, the opposite side open to the airfield runway. It was filled with more of the oil barrels and a pair of forklifts painted bright green. I ran a finger around the top of one of the barrels and took a cautious sniff. Kerosene, which is what jet fuel is.

Almost on cue, the sound of airplane engines came roaring through my earphones. The plane, a sleek silver beauty, was about a quarter-mile away. Headlights were coming from the house. I got the binoculars out. It was no pickup truck this time but a long, dark sedan. I could easily see the peace-symbol Mercedes hood ornament, but the tinted windows made the occupant invisible.

The car came to a stop a short distance from the plane. All four doors opened at the same time. A total of six people exited the car. The first one I identified was Gurbeep Singh himself, bundled up in a dark overcoat. Marta Howard was as fashionable as ever in a camel-colored, double-breasted coat. Hardev Singh was tugging at the sleeve of the man next to him, Raymond Singh. Raymond was in need of a shave and was wearing nothing but a white shirt and slacks. He was wobbling back and forth, as if he would fall down at any time. Hardev put an arm around his shoulder and pulled him toward the waiting plane.

Marta Howard was leading the pack, blond hair streaming back from her face as she strode purposefully up the small ladder attached to the plane, disappearing inside its silvery skin. Raymond was trying to pull away from Hardev. I let the binoculars dangle from their lanyard around my neck and focused the Tracker's Ear in their direction. The noise of the jet engines drowned out most of the conversation, but I could hear Gurbeep yelling, "Get him in there, damn it. Get him in there," as he waved a hand toward the plane.

148

The other two men came to give Hardev a hand. I went back to the binoculars and saw that one of them was Pirate Beard. The other was his partner, the young man who had gone with him to investigate the peacocks. They hustled Raymond up the stairs and into the plane, the two men returning toward the Mercedes as Hardev bent down and pulled the stairs back up into the plane.

I wasn't sure just what to do. Try and stop the plane? How? Raymond looked as if he was out of it, drugged probably. It was obvious he didn't want to get on that plane. I thought of taking out my revolver and firing a shot or two in the air, maybe even one at the plane itself. All that would accomplish was to set the men in the Mercedes on me. I wondered whether Pirate Beard had the shotgun in the car.

The plane's engines roared into high gear, and the pilot began taxiing away at slow speed. Within seconds it was hurtling down the runway, then rising gracefully, plunging into the dark sky. I watched its lights until they were no longer visible. It didn't take long.

22

.

The quonset-type huts I'd seen from the balloon earlier in the day were on the opposite side of the airfield runway. There were a half-dozen large trucks parked around the huts. I kept to the shadows and followed the road that the Mercedes had taken to the house, staying as far away as possible from the rows of fruit trees, and the peacocks.

An open area covered with gravel, some twenty-five yards or so wide, separated the last rows of fruit trees from the sculpted gardens around the house. It was bathed in light from cone-shaped fixtures attached to aluminum poles. There was no way to get across the lighted area without being seen, unless I shot out all the lights. I had two choices: go back the way I had come, or gamble that nobody was watching or that no electronic sensors were attached to the light fixtures.

I ran across as fast as my nervous little legs would carry me, inwardly wincing at the crunching sounds my shoes were making in the gravel. Once across and back in the dark, I bent to one knee and waited, pressing my back into a tall Italian cypress. One minute. Two minutes. Nothing. No news was good news.

The cement pathway leading to the house was painted a

light-yellow color. A narrow channel of water, the width of a quarter, ran directly down the middle of the path. I walked on the edge, ready to jump into the neatly groomed shrubs and palm trees bordering both sides. The time for the Tracker's Ear and the binoculars was long past. They were stuffed into the backpack. The .32 revolver was in my right hand, the flashlight in the left.

I had expected a moat, but there was just a narrow pool, its dark water topped by water lilies. I could hear loud laughter coming from inside the house. I skirted around the pool and through opened sliding glass doors into the house itself. There was more laughter, but coming from a distance.

I was in what must have been the living room. The inside walls were of rough stucco that had been whitewashed, then given a quick going-over in dull orange, the effect being a sherbet-like look. The couch along the wall was lemon-yellow and adorned with purple, pink, and red cushions with Arabic patterns. The floor was uneven, full of undulations like a putting green, and covered with a tightly woven beige carpet that gave you the feeling that you were looking at sand. Hip-high cement-aggregate flowerpots, filled with glossy, big-leafed green plants, were scattered around the room.

I tiptoed through a long, narrow hallway painted lime green and studded with oils and watercolors of exotic-looking flowers in elaborate gold baroque-style frames. The laughter was closer now: two voices, both male, enjoying each other's company. A curving stairway, the outside handrail of elaborately carved dark wood and a thin piece of hemp rope strung through brass holders on the opposite wall, led the way upstairs.

I peeked at my watch. Jane would be calling the police in a little over ten minutes. It could take me days to search upstairs, and I wasn't sure what I was looking for anyway. The voices got louder. I ducked into the first available door, closing it gently but leaving it open just a crack. I could hear footsteps approaching, and more laughter. Pirate Beard's young partner came sauntering by, carrying a full bottle of champagne in his hand and taking a swig right from the bottle, then wiping his sleeve across his mouth. He gave a loud burp as he disappeared down the hall.

152

I ran the flashlight beam around the room: desks, chairs, office equipment. I checked the hallway, closed the door, locked it, and used the flashlight beam to find the light switch. A bank of fluorescent lights flickered to life. Ivory-colored shades and curtains covered the far wall. A teak desk of pool-table dimensions sat in the center of the room. There were four three-drawer file cabinets lined up against one wall. I tested every drawer: locked. A long, narrow table holding a computer and a printer was placed directly behind the desk. I crossed quickly to the curtains and edged the shade back. The view looked out toward the quonset buildings.

Sitting on top of the desk was a glass ice bucket in the shape of a Fred Astaire–style top hat. An empty bottle of wine turned upside down bobbed lazily in the melted ice water. Three tulip-shaped glasses, one rimmed with lipstick, sat on a silver tray. Two of the glasses were empty, one filled to the brim with champagne that looked as if it was losing its fizz.

There was just one telephone on the desk. I copied down the number on the phone's base on a piece of scratch paper, put the paper in my wallet, then dialed the number of my car phone.

"Hello," Jane answered tentatively.

"Having fun?" I asked in a whisper.

"Probably not as much as you are. Do I call the marines?"

"Hold off for a minute, but stay on the line. I'm in the wicked witch's castle. They took off in a jet a few minutes ago. Raymond Singh was with them. He didn't look happy about getting on board."

"Nick, I almost called the cops earlier. There were some weird noises. I didn't know what they were."

"Peacocks."

"Peacocks?"

"I'll explain later, Jane."

"I think we should call the cops right now."

"Hold on. I don't want to go through all this trouble and leave empty-handed." I settled the receiver gently onto the desk, then picked it up again. "Get ready to make that call. If you hear me scream, or any gunshots, don't worry about the number I gave you. Just call 911."

A complication arises with dialing 911. The system is hooked up so that the emergency operators answering the phone can automatically see the number you are calling from on the computer sitting right in front of them. The idea is that if someone who calls has a serious medical problem and can't tell the operator where he or she is, the operator can still dispatch police, firemen, or an ambulance to the scene. That certainly makes good sense.

Some people clog up the 911 lines to ask vitally important questions about the weather, why their favorite TV show was canceled, or directions to their mother-in-law's house. The authorities have been prosecuting this particularly brain-damaged portion of society, taking computer printouts of the caller's number, along with tape recordings (they tape all 911 calls), into court to prove that Mr. Retardo did indeed call three times to ask about Fido's flea problem.

I wasn't worried about fleas, but I would just as soon not have the local authorities see my car-phone number light up their board when Jane called in our little staged crisis. So I had given her the Yuba City police number listed under non-emergency calls.

I turned my attention to the computer. It was an IBM clone, a newer, more advanced model than my own. Which meant I probably couldn't work the damn thing. I found the on switch, flicked it, and listened to the machine hum and gurgle to life. A blank light-blue screen stared back at me. I punched in the commands that bring my machine to life and got nothing but exercise for my fingers. This went on for a couple of frustrating minutes.

I went back to the phone. "Still there?"

"Nowhere to go in this town after dark," Jane answered dryly.

"There's a computer here. I can't get into it." I gave her the make and model. "Any suggestions?"

"Can't you just take the disks or something?"

"Good idea," I whispered back.

There was a smoke-gray lucite floppy-disc container alongside the computer. I emptied it of fifteen or more floppy disks,

154

slipping them inside my knapsack. There was a strong possibility that all the important material I was hoping for was on the computer's internal hard disk, and my limited knowledge wouldn't allow me to get at it.

I thought about simply opening the damn machine up and pulling out the necessary components. Problem one: I didn't know what the necessary components looked like. The insides of a computer were as confusing to me as the internal organs of the human body. I didn't really want to know just what everything looked like inside of either of them. As long as they worked, it was good enough for me.

Problem two: I was running out of time, and all I had in the way of tools was a small penknife. The printer was a laser type, with the paper in a tray at the bottom of the machine. I emptied the tray of all but two or three sheets of paper, stuffing the blank pages into the rapidly filling knapsack. Then I turned the printer on so that whoever came into the office would think that both the computer and the printer had been put to use.

Problem number three: Since I wanted Gurbeep Singh to know that I had gotten into his computer system, I'd have to let Pirate Beard or one of his friends see me. Otherwise they'd come in, see the computer and printer on, and simply turn them off, assuming that their master had carelessly left them on.

I picked up the phone again. "Jane, If you don't hear from me in ten minutes, call nine-one-one." I hung up before she could answer and say something reasonable, like "Get the hell out of there right now." I turned the light off, opened the door, and peeked out. There was the sound of voices and canned laughter. Someone was watching television. I crept down the hallway, my hand around the grip of the .32 in my jacket pocket.

A realtor would probably have described that particular part of the mansion as a game room. It had a billiards table and two old-fashioned pinball machines. A dozen or more old radios, some of them wood, others of that thick, shiny plastic used in the thirties, sat on shelves fastened to a knotty-pine-paneled wall. A gum-ball dispenser had been fashioned into a fishbowl. A replica of one of those magnificent London telephone booths stood alongside a life-sized cigar-store Indian.

155

A huge-screen rear-projection color TV set was on, showing a *Cheers* repeat. Diane was giving Sam a bad time again. I had always preferred Diane to Rebecca, much to Jane's bewilderment. Pirate Beard was sitting in a red leather chair, legs sprawled out in front of him, a bottle of wine in one hand, a long, thick cigar in the other. "Good show," I said. "I've seen this one. Diane ends up on a date with Cliff the mailman."

He turned his head slowly at first, then bolted to his feet, dropping both the cigar and the wine bottle. He came at me fast, his feet skidding to a halt on the hardwood floor when I pulled out the revolver. "Easy, now, easy. Hands over your head. Turn around slowly."

He gave me a fierce growl before following my orders. I moved up behind him, digging the gun's two-inch barrel into his spine. "Where did they go?" I said. He said something I couldn't understand, then spat on the floor. What with the wine, the cigar, and his expectorate, the maid was going to have a busy time of it in the morning.

I dug the gun deeper into his back. "Where did they go? In the airplane?"

"Fuck you," he said defiantly and predictably.

"Take off your clothes," I ordered. "Everything."

He swiveled around and glared at me. I cocked the hammer of the gun and backed away a few paces.

He started with his shirt, then shoes, then pants, finally standing there with his belly hanging over stained jockey shorts. Not a pretty sight. He gave me another glare as he hitched a thumb into the shorts' elastic waistband. "No," I said hurriedly, not wanting to subject myself to an even uglier sight. "Get down on your knees.

It would have been nice to just bop him on the head and knock him out. Or use one of those silver-screen karate chops to the back of the neck that always put those oversized bullies out like a light. The problem is, you really have to know what you're doing with those karate chops. Hit them wrong and you've got a sore hand, or you break their necks. The same with bopping someone over the head with a gun butt. You can crack a skull, do permanent brain damage, or have the gun butt glance off the target, doing no damage at all. Ah, if only life were as simple as it is in the movies.

I used his sweaty chambray shirt to bind his hands behind his back, then dug through the pockets of the jeans, finding nothing but a moldy brown leather wallet and a set of car keys on a black fob with a medal medallion showing the Mercedes emblem. The wallet contained a few ten-dollar bills and pictures of young girls. Very young. Very nude. They all seemed to be of East Indian decent. No driver's license. Nothing with a name on it.

I waved the pictures under his nose. "Who are the children?"

I got the F word again. It's now used so often that it's losing all of its power to shock and will soon be showing up in dictionaries as "Once-vulgar term for sexual intercourse. Now used as descriptive adjective for everything from recipes to movie reviews, as in "fucking awesome."

Pirate Beard's nose was thick and bent slightly to the right. I tapped it lightly with the gun barrel. It didn't straighten out. He spat again, missing the floor and hitting my shoes. Macho man. If I was going to get anything out of Pirate Beard I'd have to beat it out of him.

I pushed the gun barrel into his tangled beard, shoving it around until I found the opening to his mouth. "Tell your employer that I made copies of all his files in the computer. If he wants them he'll have to pay me a lot of money. Tell him I want money and Raymond Singh alive. Can you remember all that?"

His mouth was moving around as if he wanted to bite the little barrel off the revolver. "Tell him Nick, the man he met in London, said that." I backed away as he hawked another wad of spit in my general direction.

I used the phone booth to dial my car phone again. "Call the cops yet?" I asked.

"Seconds away from dialing. You like to cut it close, don't you, Nick?"

"Relax. I'm on my way. In style. A Mercedes."

23

■

The next morning we returned the truck and the ladder and headed back to San Francisco. Jane grilled me during the drive, filling up one of those palm-sized spiral memo books that reporters like to use with an account of what had happened the night before and theories as to what we were going to do about it and how much of it she could use in a story.

The first chore was seeing what was on those floppy disks. A glance at their labels wasn't too promising: technical-data input, including DOS, software programs such as Vokswriter and Total Word, a spell-checker, a thesaurus, printer commands, tools to put the computer to work, everything but Nintendo. There were two blank disks that did look promising.

"Why not just take everything and dump it in the cops' laps?" Jane asked reasonably.

"Which cops? Back in London? The Yuba City cops? The Immigration and Naturalization Service?"

"I thought you told me that those people in London were going to get in touch with the immigration people here. I'm surprised you haven't heard from them." I was, too.

Mrs. Damonte caught us going up the stairs. She opened her

door wide, scowled at Jane, then in rapid Italian asked me whether we had gone to Reno. Reno is the Bay Area's answer to Las Vegas, where people slip away to get married in those seedy little chapels with the piped-in organ music. I assured her that such was not the case, and she lifted her eyebrows a millimeter, which for Mrs. D. is the equivalent of the makeup-cracking smiles you see on the Miss America contestants.

"What does "Reno" mean in Italian?" Jane asked, once we were inside my flat.

"Reno?"

"Yes. I thought that was what Mrs. Damonte said."

"Oh, yeah. It's a guy's name. Joe Reno. Friend of hers who was sick. She was just telling me he's all right now."

In her line of work Jane has faced some pretty rough customers—juvenile-minded, oversexed athletes; prima donnas of show business; hardline cops; and just general nogoodniks—and survived without a scratch. But she's tongue-tied and intimidated whenever she gets in sight of Mrs. Damonte. You couldn't call it a feminine reaction, because the same thing happens to me.

I started the coffee going. Then we went into my office and played with the computer disks, "played" being the operative word. The labeled disks were just what they said they were, therefore useless. The unlabeled disks also turned out to be useless: sex-game disks, something I didn't even know existed. The characters were unrealistically drawn. The tall, blond woman's figure would have had to clock in at something around forty-four–sixteen–thirty-five in real life. The men—there were four of them—had penises that, if pointed down—which they never were—would have dragged on the floor. There was a format you could use to position the playing partners just where you wanted them, like directing your own porno movie.

"That's disgusting," Jane said, after a couple of minutes' viewing.

The second disk didn't last a full minute after we determined that the cast of characters were an elongated woman in a leather Batgirl-type outfit, a curly moppet in a French maid's uniform, and a German shepherd.

"Not exactly *Sesame Street*," I said, dropping both disks into the wastebasket. "Unless my bluff works out, and Gurbeep Singh thinks I copied all the files in the computer, and unless there is something in those files he is worried about, the trip to Yuba City was a flop."

"It wasn't a flop. At least you saw Raymond Singh and know he's alive," Jane assured me.

True. Raymond was alive, at least when he got on the airplane. I wondered how thick the bond between the two cousins was. Gurbeep could drop Raymond's body out of the plane somewhere over the Pacific Ocean, and it would never be found, except by the sharks.

"They'll call, Nick," Jane said. "I bet they'll call."

I was so anxious to check the computer disks that I hadn't even looked at my telephone-answering machine. The little box that listed the number of calls that had come in since yesterday showed the number seven.

Six of the calls were identical, a small, nervous, young female voice saying, "I'll call back." Just that and nothing more. The seventh call was from an insurance adjuster who was a client of mine.

"Who's the scared little girl?" inquired Jane.

"Regina. Raymond's cousin. The one who works at his store."

I called the insurance adjuster while Jane went to pour coffee. I could hear her rummaging through the refrigerator. My continued bachelor status had softened up Mrs. Damonte so much that she brought us lunch, a frittata made with eggs, garlic, anchovies, Romano cheese, and fresh tomatoes. Mrs. D. stayed long enough to share a glass of wine with us and wait for our rave reviews of the frittata. Jane accurately told her that it was delicious, wonderful, fantastic. Mrs. D. accepted the adulation with her usual stone face. Upon leaving she gave me her oft-repeated description of Jane, which, roughly translated, was "Too skinny. Won't make good babies."

"What was that Mrs. Damonte said?" Jane asked, after Mrs. D. was safely out the door. I was saved having to reply by the ringing of the phone. As I went to answer it, the doorbell started chiming. Jane volunteered to go to the door.

161

"Is that you, Mr. Polo?" asked the timid voice on the phone.

"Regina?"

There was a long pause before she said, "Yes, it is me."

"Have you heard from Raymond?" I asked.

"No. No. Not a word. I am sorry I ran away the other night. I want to talk to you. Can you come to talk to me?"

"Sure. Where are you?"

"No police!" she shouted.

"No," I promised her. "No police."

She gave me an address in the six-hundred block of Hyde Street. "Apartment Eleven-forty-five." I agreed to meet her in an hour.

Jane was standing in the front room, talking to a tall, trim black man in his forties. His hair was cut close to his head, just starting to show gray at the temples. He was dressed in a gray herringbone business suit, baggy at the knees. "This is Jake Simpson of the Immigration and Naturalization Service," Jane announced.

Simpson cleared his throat, like a man with a cold coming on. "Howdy." His handshake was marshmallow-soft, but I got the feeling that he could put a lot of muscle into it if the need arose.

"Sit down, Mr. Simpson," I said, pointing to the couch near the front windows. "How can I help you?"

Simpson settled down, plopped his briefcase on his lap, opened it, and pulled out a sheaf of papers. "A Clive Turner of the Foreign Office of Great Britain contacted us. Regarding an Oliver Trent and Carlisle, Inc."

"You're familiar with Trent and Carlisle?" I asked.

Jane sat down in the leather chair next to the stereo. She leaned forward, hugging her knees. She was wearing those white shorts again. Simpson gave Jane a long look, but not because of her legs.

"Ms. Tobin is a good friend," I said. "And a reporter for the Bulletin."

"So she told me," Simpson said, looking skeptical.

162

"Everything is off the record, as far as I'm concerned," Jane volunteered.

"We've heard of Trent. And Carlisle," Simpson finally said. "What can you tell me about them?"

I gave him the short version of the story: that I'd been hired by a local merchant, Raymond Singh, to deliver a package to his cousin, Gurbeep Singh, in London.

"Yes, yes," Simpson said, shuffling through his papers. "I have the reports here. Chief Inspector Carter says there was a homicide."

I told him briefly about the events that had taken place in London, adding nothing that I was sure wasn't in those reports from Clive Turner and Inspectors Carter and Mandel.

Simpson put all of his papers back in his briefcase, closed it with a snap, then leaned back on the sofa. "And what did your client, Raymond Singh, say when you came back home?"

"Haven't been able to find him," I said.

"Haven't seen him?" queried Simpson.

"Haven't been able to say a single word to him." Which was true. I would have had to shout over the blasts of those jet engines for Raymond to hear me. "He seems to have disappeared."

Simpson leaned forward and stared at me hard. "What do you think happened to him?"

I shrugged a shoulder. "I don't know. I told the London police that I didn't believe that Raymond Singh was involved in smuggling aliens. I still think that, though I wouldn't bet my life on it. What do you think?"

Simpson put the briefcase on the ground and casually looped one leg over the other. "Those people in London weren't very impressed with you, Mr. Polo. You got better reviews from the local cops."

"Who'd you talk to?" I asked.

"Bob Tehaney." Tehaney was a homicide inspector I knew well.

"You know how many men we've got working at the INS?"

I turned my palms up. "No idea."

Simpson snorted. "Not enough. Not nearly enough. The

Mexicans, the Salvadorans, they get all the ink in the papers. Over a million a year cross the border. Coyotes. That's what they call the men who bring them across." He turned his eyes on Jane. "Floods of them. Literally floods of them. If we arrest them, they go back across the border. Next day they're coming back. Wears you down." He smacked his lips. "Wouldn't have a cup of coffee handy, would you?"

We moved into the kitchen, and I started another pot of coffee. Simpson took off his suit coat and draped it over the back of one of the kitchen chairs. The gun on his hip was a big automatic. We made small talk until the coffee was ready.

"Yes, the Latinos get all the ink, but we're having a lot of trouble up north too. That's how the Asians and East Indians get in: Canada, down through Washington and Oregon, into California. There are gangs that specialize: bring in your family, bring in men for working the fields, women for cleaning, for prostitution." He took a sip of the coffee and smiled. "That's good coffee. Real good. Ever hear of NAMBLA, Mr. Polo, Ms. Tobin?"

Jane wrinkled her forehead at the acronym. "The North American Man/Boy Love Association," I said.

"Exactly," Simpson agreed. "An organization of men, mostly white men, whose goal is to legalize sexual relations between men and boys. Very young boys. They take them in as young as three and four. Keep them until they get old. Real old. Thirteen or so. Trade them back and forth like rare postage stamps."

"God, that's sick," Jane said.

"Most of these NAMBLA people are wealthy. They run the organization like a secret government agency. Computers with coded access. Meetings and conventions. They're the worse kind of sickos, Miss Tobin. They believe in what they're doing. Think they're helping these little babies. Introducing them to the good life." Simpson stared into the bottom of his empty coffee cup as if perhaps its contents could explain life's mysteries.

I said, "So you're saying that Carlisle, Inc., is involved in supplying boys to NAMBLA."

164

"Oh, yeah." He pointed a finger at Jane. "But I'm not saying that for publication."

"Perhaps a story on NAMBLA would do some good," Jane argued. "I'm not sure a lot of people even know it exists."

Simpson bobbed his head. "You could be right. Or the story could just increase its membership. Lot of weirdos out there who would probably want to join up. NAMBLA's not the only problem. There are other organizations, just as powerful and just as rotten as NAMBLA, that specialize in young girls." His dark eyes had a moist sheen when they turned on me. "From what we know of Carlisle, Inc., they supply them all. Little boys and little girls, relatives, laborers. That's the kind of people you're mixed up with, Mr. Polo."

24

.

"You didn't volunteer much information," Jane snapped at me, once the broad shoulders of Jake Simpson were out my front door.

"That telephone call," I explained. "From little Regina. She wants to talk. But no cops. She's still scared as hell of anyone involved with law enforcement."

The address Regina had given me was a typical multi-unit apartment house built in the 1920s on the outer fringes of the tenderloin district, near Saint Francis's Hospital. Two young women dressed in hospital whites were exiting through the building's front door while I was buzzing Regina's apartment on the intercom.

She sounded nervous and jumpy when she asked my name. She opened her door a crack. I could see her eyes widen at the sight of Jane. "My associate," I told the frightened girl. Jane arched her eyebrows at the job description, but we had agreed that Regina would no doubt be as wary of reporters as she was of cops.

"No police?" Regina questioned.

"No. Can we come in?"

167

The sour smell of years of unvented cooking permeated the apartment. The room we were in was crowded with old uphol- stered chairs and couches of various colors and patterns. A brown-and-beige braided rug covered what little unoccupied floor space there was. There were a half-dozen paintings on the wall, the cream of the crop being one of Elvis on a velvet background.

I could see the kitchen through an open door. A heavyset woman in her sixties, dark hair in a bun, was stirring a pot on the stove with a wooden spoon. "That's my mother," Regina said, plopping down into one of the chairs.

"Regina. What a pretty name," Jane said, sitting down across from the girl.

"Not my real name," she admitted sheepishly. "But I like it. It sounds romantic."

"What is your real name?" Jane asked.

"Vilma," she said, with a wrinkling of her nose.

"That's pretty too," Jane told her.

The woman in the kitchen stared at us, all the while stirring her pot. "Don't worry about her," Regina said. "She can't speak English."

I leaned against the wall, alongside Elvis. "Did your mother come over here to America with you?"

She bolted to her feet, then abruptly sat down again, hands on her thighs, eyes fixed on the floor. "We came together. With the others."

"Which others?"

She parried my question with one of her own. "Have you found Raymond?"

"No," I said. "But I saw him. Briefly. Up in Yuba City. Do you know where that is?"

She tilted her head up to look at me, a hand pushing the hair from the front of her face. "Yuba City? No."

"It's over a hundred miles from here. Farmland. Orchards. Raymond owns property there. So does a man with the last name of Sidhu. Do you know him?"

A shake of the head.

"Gurbeep Singh was there. Raymond's cousin."

Another shake of the head.

"Hardev was there. The man from the boat."

"The man who raped you," Jane added.

Regina brought her small hands together in a clap. "Bastard," she said.

"Raymond was with these people," I said. "But he looked as if he was drugged. As if he wanted to get away. They put him on an airplane. A small, private jet."

She bolted up again, bent her head down, and spat at the rug. "Drugs. Yes, they always use drugs. They did that to me on the boat."

Jane rose and slowly put a hand out toward Regina. "Is that how you got to America? On the boat?"

Regina nodded her head vigorously. "Yes. The plane, the boat, the plane, then the boat. The bad boat." Her face went though some subtle changes in a manner of moments, the end result being that she suddenly looked much older, much sadder.

"I'm grateful to Raymond for bringing us here." Her eyes drifted toward the woman in the kitchen. "For bringing both of us here. You don't know what it was like at home. Bad. Very bad. We are *Harijans*. The men are pigs. All of them. Especially the police. One policeman, a pig like Hardev, raped eighteen women." She pointed a finger at her chest. "Girls. Like me. Younger. Eighteen of us. The judge, another pig, he released the policeman. Do you know why? Do you know why?" The second question was double the volume of the first. "Because," she continued, on the verge of tears, "the judge said the women were so poor that they could have been bribed to make a false charge against the policeman. Pigs."

"That's awful," Jane said, wrapping an arm around Regina's heaving shoulders and gently helping her back down onto the chair. "Why did Raymond bring you to America?" Jane asked softly.

"My mother wrote to him. Raymond is a good man. Like a father to me. We try to pay him back. He has helped many people. Many. He is trying to get Iqbal and Amrik, my cousins. They are only babies, five and six. Raymond is trying to get them to America." She looked up at me. "That is why he sent you to London, I think. To get Iqbal and Amrik."

"Are they still in India?" Jane asked.

She shook her head. "I don't know. Raymond doesn't tell me everything. He was mad, very mad, that I didn't tell him about what happened on the boat when I first came here."

Jane crouched down so that she was eye level with the girl. "Did anyone else hurt you on the boat?"

"Oh, yes. Men. Strange men I had never seen before."

"What about your mother?" Jane asked. "Where was she?"

"They only kept me, another girl younger than me, and two little boys." She held a hand up to indicate the boys' heights. "Little boys. We were the only ones on the boat."

"I thought you said your mother came with you," I said, wondering just how reliable Regina's story was.

"Oh, yes, on the airplane and the other boat. But not the bad boat. The big, fancy one. That's where they lived. On the fancy boat. What do you call it? A ya—"

"A yacht? It was a yacht?"

She flashed a small smile. "Yes. Very big. Very grand. Not like the other. That was old. Stinky. My mother and five or six others, we were jammed into rooms. The plane was old, too, not nice," she rolled a hand in front of her, searching for the right words. "Like cattle. We were like cattle then."

I kneeled alongside Jane and stared into Regina's fear-glazed eyes. "This boat. You say they lived there? Who lived there?"

"The men. The man who made sex with me. And the others."

"How long were you on this boat?" Jane asked.

"Not long, I think. I'm not sure." She ran a finger along the inner part of her left arm. "Drugs. They gave us drugs in needles. But I don't think it was too long. Maybe a few days. Maybe a week."

"And the boat was where?" I asked. "In America?"

Her eyes closed halfway, her forehead corrugating in thought. "No. North. Canada."

Jane said, "Was it Vancouver?"

"Beautiful water. Many ships. I could see many buildings

170

from the boat's windows. At night. The boat had big windows, like a house." She nodded her head toward the windows looking out on Hyde Street. "Like those," she said, then twirled a finger in front of our faces. "The top of one building went around. Like that."

I took out the photograph Raymond had given me showing himself and Gurbeep Singh. "Was this man there?" I asked Regina, handing her the picture.

"Yes! He was there. He was like the—the boss, I guess you'd say. They were all nice to him. Raymond showed me his picture, after I told him what happened."

Jane said, "Did he assault you, too?"

Regina's pretty face slowly worked its way into a snarl. "No. He liked the boys. Little boys like Iqbal and Amrik. Raymond said that he would make sure that they would not be hurt."

"This is important," I told her. "Very important. What can you remember about the boat?"

"Oh, it was big. Beautiful. Everything there was beautiful. Except the men."

"You never got a look at the name, did you, Regina? It's usually painted on the side of the boat."

"They never let us see outside. Our eyes were covered up, blindfolded. But once some of the men took me into a big room, with a table and chairs and lots of beautiful furniture. There were many pictures of a boat on the wall. The pictures showed the outside and the inside of the boat, and the pictures of the inside looked just like that room, so I think it was the same boat. It had a beautiful name: *Ramayana*."

Regina gave me her home phone number, and I had her draw a sketch of the *Ramayana*. She gave me a timid handshake and Jane a light kiss on the cheek as we left.

"Have you been to Vancouver?" Jane asked once we were back in my car.

"No." I waited until a bakery truck lumbered down Hyde Street before swinging into traffic. "But it looks as if I may be making a trip."

171

"There's a Sheraton Hotel that has a revolving restaurant on top. It looks right out into the harbor."

The bakery truck double-parked. The driver leaned out the door to talk to a tall transvestite hooker in a pink miniskirt. The two lanes alongside the truck were bumper to bumper, and none of the drivers looked as if they'd let me nudge into their lane. I beeped the horn, getting a glare and a middle-digit wave from the hooker. She had bleached-blond hair, and even at this distance I could see dark hair glistening around her chin.

"Do you think that the boat would still be up there?" Jane said, returning the working boy/girl's wave.

"Who knows? I'll have to try and track it down. Vancouver looks like the connection, though."

"I feel so sorry for Regina."

"Me too." The bakery driver handed the hooker a few loaves of bread, then took off in a puff of dirty exhaust. Blondie placed one of the loaves of bread in a strategic position and waved it like a phallic symbol as we drove by. Ah, the charms of San Francisco.

"At least it sounds as if Raymond Singh is off the hook, Nick."

"Yes." That was a relief. Raymond had turned out to be one of the good guys, after all, if you discount a few federal crimes such as smuggling in relatives. But he got them jobs, took care of them when they got here, and, if Regina could be believed, and I certainly hoped she could, didn't participate in any of the child-sex games that Gurbeep and his crowd were into.

I turned right on Ellis Street. Though it was early and there was a misty fog dampening the pavement and the hopes of the retirees who had nowhere else to live, the drug-dealers and multisex hookers were out in packs.

"I could use a drink, Nick."

"Me too. Let's stop at my place. Maybe there's been a call from those bastards, and I can get started on running down that boat."

I was in the curb lane, getting ready to make a right turn onto Larkin and wind my way back to North Beach. Suddenly something huge pulled alongside and jolted the Ford, pushing us

172

to the curb lane. I slammed on the brakes, jabbed at the horn button, and tried to keep from skidding into the cars parked directly to the right, but whatever it was that had gotten hold of us was a force unto itself.

I looked out the side window, but all I could see was a mass of black metal. The side of the car where Jane was sitting was being forced against the parked cars. We were being pulled along at a frightening speed. Directly up ahead was a double-parked vehicle, the familiar dark brown of a United Parcel Service truck. If I couldn't pull free or get the Ford to stop, we were going to crash right into the rear of the truck.

There was nothing but noise, the screeching of metal, the sound of the tires digging into the wet pavement, Jane screaming, me shouting, engines roaring. My feet were so far down on the brake petal that I was raised up from the seat, my head bouncing on the roof. We were being squeezed together like an accordion. The last thing I remember was intuition taking over and turning off the car's motor as we plowed into the back of the UPS truck.

25

.

They call them "the jaws of life," a dramatic description for a set of connecting pieces of hardware of various sizes and shapes operated by a pneumatic pump. The firemen who used them were experts, and they began peeling away my car piece by piece.

Jane said that she was feeling all right, but there was blood coming from her forehead, and she kept passing out. It seemed to take hours, as it always does at a time like that, but later I examined the fire-department reports and found that they had been notified of the crash by the owner of a nearby dry-cleaning store, had arrived on the scene within three minutes, and had gotten Jane out of the car in eight minutes and me eleven minutes later.

Jane went right onto a stretcher, into an ambulance, and off to the hospital. Since I was relatively free of injuries, they saved me for last. Two smiling-faced firemen, helmets tilted back, joked with me as they carefully went through the procedure of working me out of the metal jigsaw puzzle that had once been my car.

I don't know what the car's width was before the accident, but it looked about half of its original size, all scrunched in. One of the firemen, a tall Filipino with the name Wilson stenciled on his turnout coat, told me just how lucky we were. "Another eight or nine inches and you would have had the motor sitting on your lap and the steering wheel through your chest, brother." He held out his hands a short distance apart. "That much more and you would have been all squashed to pieces."

They had knocked out what remained of the front windshield and pulled Jane out through the opening. For me they had to work their way through the twisted mess of the left-side rear door. I felt like a first-round knockout victim when I finally got free and was standing on the street.

The fireman named Wilson patted me on the back. "No gas. Good thing you turned the engine off. If there'd been a fire you'd both be cooked by now. Your girlfriend looks like she's going to be okay. Concussion, maybe. Right arm looks like it's broken, but no internal injuries that we could see." I thanked Wilson and his crew, making a note of the number on the side of the fire engine so that I could send them a proper thank-you card inside a case of good whiskey.

I didn't know the traffic cop who took the report. We sat in his patrol car and I gave him what little information I had. "Name?" the cop asked.

"Nick Polo." I hadn't realized my hand was shaking so badly until I tried digging my badge out of my pants. Once he knew I was an ex-cop things went smoothly.

"Got a call a few minutes ago. Abandoned big rig down on Van Ness. Paint scrapes all along the right side, beige, like your buggy. Belongs to an outfit called Eckstein Trucking down in South San Francisco. They say it must have been swiped out of their yard. They had nobody working up here today. I'll check it out. One witness on the street, looks like a hype, so I don't know how much I believe him, says he got a look at the driver of the truck. Dark guy with a beard."

I thanked him, and he took the rest of the report on the way to San Francisco General Hospital. If you've seen the Steve McQueen movie *Bullitt*, you'll remember SF General as an old red-brick building where McQueen has a foot-chase after one of the baddies. It hasn't changed much since the movie. The bricks are a little grimier, the rooms a lot more crowded, but if you're unlucky enough to get into a serious accident in San Francisco, then pray that you're lucky enough to get sent to SF General's Trauma Center. The doctors and nurses there are miracle-workers, much too reminiscent of a MASH unit, their war being the streets of San Francisco. They toil away at a never-ending line of customers suffering from gunshot wounds, stabbings, third-degree burns, or sporting injuries resulting from the current street vogue, beating victims to a pulp with aluminum baseball bats.

I wondered just how long the big rig had been following us. Had they picked us up right after we had left little Regina's apartment? Could she be in on it, after all? If not, she was in danger. I showed my police badge to a harried nurse, and she let me use the phone at her station desk.

Regina picked up the phone on the first ring. I told her what had happened. There was no way to read her response. Just silence. "If they followed me from your place, Regina, they may know what apartment you're in. It might be a good idea for you and your mother to move for a couple of days. Do you have some friends you can stay with?"

"Yes. We will be all right."

"Okay. Call me if there are any problems."

Before hanging up, she said in her soft little voice, "I hope you and your lady friend are all right."

A bright-faced young doctor in a blood-spattered green smock introduced himself as Dr. Hamilton and told me that my lady friend was going to be fine. His diagnosis was almost exactly the same as the fireman's: concussion and a fracture of the right ulna, which he patiently explained was the forearm. His medical advice was that Jane was resting comfortably and would be upstairs in her room but should not have any visitors for an hour or so. He gave me a quick once-over. "You don't look so hot yourself."

Actually, I *was* hot. Hot under the collar. Hot at Gurbeep Singh and all his lousy henchmen. "Dark man with a beard" was the only description of the driver of the truck that had crushed us. The odds on his being Pirate Beard from Yuba City looked better than even money to me.

177

Dazed and muddled as I was, I had enough sense not to go searching for the hospital cafeteria. Across the street, on Potrero, was a delicatessen, Jeff's Ready-to-Go Sandwiches. The special of the day was turkey, ham, and Swiss cheese on a crusty sourdough roll. I took my sandwich and Coke outside and leaned against a telephone pole, my eyes watching the passing traffic. The sandwich was good. When I finished, I went back and got another, knowing Jane was not going to be happy with whatever food the hospital was providing.

She was lying in bed in a room jammed with six more beds, all occupied by heavily bandaged women. I closed the thin avocado-green curtain around Jane's bed and waited for her to wake up. The conversations of the other patients and their visitors that drifted through the thin curtain were mostly in Spanish.

Jane's head was wrapped in a turban of bandages. Her arm was set in plaster. I held her free hand, my index finger on her wrist, feeling a strong, steady beat. It was almost seven when her eyes started flickering, looking confused at first as she squinted at me. Even raising an eyebrow appeared to cause her pain.

She mumbled a few unintelligible words, then looked at her arm in the cast. "Damn, that hurts," she said, then fluttered her lips and gave me a slight smile. "What time is it?" she asked, her voice strained and hoarse.

"Seven o'clock."

She swiveled her head, seeing nothing but the light-green curtain. "Day or night?"

"Night."

"They serve dinner already?"

I picked up the delicatessen bag from the floor and took out the sandwich. "My hero," Jane sighed, reaching for the food with her good hand.

The doctor, a tall serious-faced woman in her forties, came by about a half-hour later and gave Jane a detailed report. They expected no complications with either her head injury or the broken arm. "You'll be with us a couple of days, Ms. Tobin," the doctor said, "unless you've got private coverage and want to move to another hospital." You go to San Francisco General

Hospital for their emergency services. Then you get out as soon as possible.

"Yes, I have coverage," Jane said. "I do want to transfer."

"I understand perfectly," the doctor said with a smile. She looked at the remains of the sandwich, then turned her eyes on me. "You get that at Jeff's deli?"

"Right," I said.

"Good move," she said with a sparkle in her eyes for the first time. "The food here can kill you."

I stayed with Jane for another hour. A hospital administrator with a thick armload of forms came by. While they completed the necessary paperwork, I found a pay phone down the hall.

I get squeamish in hospitals. Always have. Worse than in funeral parlors. Can't help it. My vital organs tighten up and my voice goes dry. All those poor battered, broken, carved-up bodies struggling to make it through another day. Maybe it's because I feel that somewhere out there there's a hospital bed with my name on it. Sooner or later, much later, I hope, it will get me, tangle me up in tubes and electrodes, and I'll lie there waiting, watching my heartbeat flutter across a screen, the little pyramidal line of each heartbeat getting smaller and smaller until it ends in that final straight line.

Of course, if Gurbeep Singh and his cronies had their way, I wouldn't have to worry about dying in a hospital bed anymore. They had much more exotic plans for the remains of one Nicholas Polo.

I dialed my answering machine. No messages. I dug the telephone number for the Sidhu property up in Yuba City out of my wallet. I used my credit card to call the number. The click of an answering machine was followed by a deep, resonant voice that said, "Leave the time of your call and the nature of your business, please."

"The nature of my business is that I'm going to burn your asses, you bastards. You think I was kidding about running off those figures on your computer? A lot of information there. I was talking to a man from the INS. You know, the Immigration and Naturalization Service. He told me some interesting stories

179

about smuggling kids out of India. Young kids. Selling them to people like those fruitcakes from NAMBLA. I bet he'd be interested in your computer material. But he wouldn't pay for it, would he? Your try at killing me today just upped the ante. And say hello to Raymond for me. He looked a little shaky getting on your plane. I want Raymond alive and healthy. Just call and set up an appointment. And get ready to spend some money. Big money."

26

.

I hitched a ride on the ambulance that transported Jane down to Seton Hospital in Daly City, just a couple of foggy miles south of the San Francisco border. The rooms were much cleaner, the smell less antiseptic, the staff cheerful and professional, but it was still a hospital, and I took off as soon as Jane was settled into her new, starchy white sheets. "Bring something for breakfast" were her last words before she drifted off to sleep.

I cabbed it to the airport, where I was sure I could find a car-rental agency open for business. The taxi driver must have thought that I was under treatment for some rare twitching disease, because I kept looking over my shoulder for a tail. I drove the rented Ford with less than four hundred miles on the odometer back into town the hard way, out Skyline Boulevard, through a dark and foggy Golden Gate Park that would have brought good cheer to Mike, the London cabby. It looked like an ideal ideal spot for a ripper movie.

By the time I popped out of the park and onto Oak Street, I was sure no one was following me. Dark and deserted parks are an ideal way of picking up tails. It's also an ideal place for a someone tailing you to zero in and perform whatever nasty deeds he has in mind. Of course, all that fancy dodging around wouldn't do me much good if someone was waiting a half-block from my flat with a high-powered rifle.

I parked in the driveway, cursing myself for leaving the garage-door-opener in my wrecked car. Rather than make myself an inviting target by opening the garage manually, I left the car where it was and ran up the front steps. It was past midnight now, and Mrs. Damonte was missing from her sentry post.

I gave the door a good eye-check before sticking the key into the lock, though if a professional with a bomb had been playing games with the lock he wouldn't have left a trace visible to the naked eye. The latest twist in plastic explosives is packaging them in tubes of caulking, like the kind used to seal cracks around windows and steps. That way, a sophisticated terrorist can buy his tubes of DuPont C6 or the Czechoslovakian-made Semtex and simply spread the potent explosive in a neat, trim line around your doors, windows, and floorboards.

There was certainly nothing sophisticated about the way Pirate Beard had tried to crush my car, but once you've been made a target by a killer, your mind considers every possible method that may be used against you. I gave the flat a complete shakedown before going to bed. And yes, I did look under the bed before lying down. If I'd had a teddy bear I'd have hugged it all night. After checking it for explosives, of course.

The phone woke me up a little after six. "Mr. Polo?" The voice was calm, cultured, that slight British upper-class accent.

"Speaking."

"I received your message. I have no idea what you are talking about. Did someone try to kill you?"

"Is this Gurbeep?" I asked.

"Please, no names. I did understand the part about your having some information from a computer. Information you stole, after breaking into and entering someone else's property. That is the right charge, isn't it? Breaking and entering?"

"You should know more than me about what to call criminal offenses," I said. "The material is going to be expensive."

"How expensive?" he asked, the voice purring along in those well-modulated tones.

182

"A half-million."

"Half a million? Are you joking?"

"No. That's the price now. In dollars. You wait around another day and I'll make it pounds."

"That is out of the question, I'm afraid."

"Then I'll drop it in the lap of the INS. Or send it to Mr. Clive Turner of the British Foreign Office or Chief Inspector Carter of Scotland Yard. All of this will cost me a lot of postage, but it'll be worth it. I can write the stamps off, claim them as a business expense."

There was no response. "How's Raymond?" I added. "His friends, his attorney, his wife, and the local cops might all like to know that when I last saw him being hustled aboard a sexy little silver jet plane, Raymond didn't look too happy about getting on board. The pictures turned out well. I'm sure that if I have them blown up you'll all look good. Tell Marta Howard she looks absolutely smashing."

Another long pause. "Pictures, you say?"

"You don't think I hopped over that fence just to play with your peacocks and ransack your house, do you? Of course I took pictures," I lied confidently, because it was something that a bright, well-trained investigator would have done. Too bad I hadn't thought of it.

"Perhaps we should meet," he answered, after yet another long pause. "Come to Vancouver. I'll reserve a room for you at the Pacific Hotel. Come as soon as possible. I'm sure you'd like to speak to Raymond. In fact, if you don't come, he'll be heartbroken. At the very least, heartbroken. I'm sure we can do business, Mr. Polo." He hung up before I could respond to his nicely worded threat against Raymond Singh's life. The phone rang again. "And bring everything with you, Mr. Polo," said the man who didn't want to use his name on the phone. "Everything."

"They're delicious," Jane said, struggling to a sitting position and making short work of one of the "dead-bones" cookies I'd picked up at Victoria Pastry. She looked a lot better: color back in her cheeks, sparkle in her eyes when she wasn't wincing,

183

lips making smacking noises as she worked her way through the cookies.

"When are they going to release you?" I asked, risking a slap on the hands by going for one of the cookies, delicious little concoctions of meringue topped with hazelnuts.

"Tomorrow morning, probably." Her face turned serious. "What about those people? Have you heard from them?"

I reached for her glass of milk, taking a big sip to help wash down the remains of the cookie. "Early this morning. I've been invited to Vancouver."

"You're not going, are you, Nick? What about the police? Have you called Jake Simpson at the INS?"

"Yes, no, and no," I responded in order to her questions. "I am going. No cops. Yet." I looked around her room. There was only one bed, stripped down to its mattress, against the opposite wall. "I'd feel better if you were somewhere a little more protected than you are here."

"They're not after *me*, Nick," Jane said while working her mouth around another cookie. "But I still think you're crazy for not going to the cops. I liked that Jake Simpson. He looked"— she rolled her eyes toward the ceiling while searching for the right description—"solid, trustworthy."

"I agree. He's also overworked and understaffed. If Gurbeep and his crew smell any cops, they'll simply scuttle everything. Including my client, Raymond Singh. No. I like Simpson too. And I'll call him. But after I take a peek at Vancouver."

Jane tossed me a cookie, like a winner at a roulette wheel rewarding a croupier. "I won't go into any long discourse about what you should or shouldn't do, Nick, but remember, I've got an interest in this, too. A story. And I was almost killed. So I want you to do me one favor before you leave."

"You have but to ask," I said graciously.

The pain on her face was obvious as she maneuvered herself into a sitting position, then pushed her injured arm in my direction. "Sign my cast."

I had already packed a suitcase, so I just had to make a stop at a magic-supply store on Mission Street, then head for the

184

airport. The airline had assured me that flights took off for Seattle every hour on the hour, not counting unusual delays, of course. Maybe they didn't count them, but I and my fellow passengers did, a total of forty-two minutes of delays.

I kept eyeing all the people milling around at the gates, not really expecting to see any of Gurbeep's boys but just out of general curiosity. Airport terminals are turning into premier people-watching places, partly because a lot of deals go on there: drug deals. Money exchanges. The actual transfer of narcotics takes place somewhere else. One of the participants uses his cellular phone or an airport pay phone to maneuver his part of the deal, while the other uses his phone to have his partners go to the designated pickup spot. No drugs change hands at the airport, but money does. Lots of money.

Why airports? Because the two main honchos know that the other guy, and anyone with him, is unarmed. No one who wanted to stay in business very long would risk trying to get a gun through those airport metal detectors. But money, tapped to the body or stuffed into pockets, passes through without a problem. And after the transfer, the man who ends up with the money can just hop on a plane and fly away.

They finally announced that my flight was boarding. I was back where I belonged, in the tourist section of a United Airlines 737. Tourist was certainly nothing like first class, but considering the cost of the flight—$218 round trip in tourist class, $699 one way in first class—it would have to do.

We got into Seattle early in the evening. I waited for my suitcase at the luggage carousel. Luckily, the airline didn't check the cargo baggage through a metal detector, because my little black bag consisted of an overabundance of shirts and underwear wrapped around a .38 Magnum, the .32 revolver, and reams of flash paper.

I rented a car and, following the pert rental agent's instructions, maneuvered my way onto the interstate highway and headed north. The weather was cool and gray, just as it had been in London, just as it is much of the time in San Francisco. For someone who was doing a fair amount of traveling, I certainly wasn't seeing many climatic changes.

185

It was some seventy miles to Vancouver, a nice, scenic little drive. The border-patrol guards were neatly dressed and polite, waving me through after a few brief questions. I got a glimpse of the large white arch in Peace Arch Park. Then, a few minutes later, I was in downtown Vancouver.

Gurbeep had booked me into the Pacific Hotel, the same hotel that Raymond Singh had originally been scheduled to stay at, according to his travel agent, Gloria Perret. My tour guide gave the Pacific five stars. I chose something just a little less grand and two blocks from the Pacific, the three-star New World Harborside Hotel on Seymour Street, which had, among its many other attractions, a revolving restaurant, called Vistas on the Bay, on the twentieth floor.

After checking in, I went right up to the restaurant. Regina had said that she had looked out of a window on the boat and seen a building with a top that turned around. The bartender confirmed Jane's information that the nearby Sheraton Landmark Hotel also had a revolving top floor. Regina could have been looking at either structure.

I sipped at an iced Stolichnaya and looked out at Vancouver Harbor. Beautiful. And big. And crowded. The lights from dozens and dozens of boats of all sizes and shapes crisscrossed the dark waters of the bay. Was the *Ramayana* out there somewhere? I had checked every available nautical database under that name but had come up with nothing. The boat could have been registered in some foreign country or a state other than Washington and California. Or Regina simply could have had the name wrong. A big yacht, black sides, white sails, and windows instead of portholes. How hard could it be to find a boat like that?

Dinner was a delicious salmon steak and fettuccine that would have received a nod of approval from Mrs. Damonte. After coffee, the white-jacketed waiter asked whether I needed anything else.

"Just a yacht."

"You and me both, sir," he said, handing me the bill. "You and me both."

I walked off dinner in the company of the last of the Cuban cigars I'd pilfered from Raymond Singh's office. The expensive

186

smoke billowing up into the cool Vancouver evening air must have given the hot-pants-and-leather-boots prostitutes down by the waterfront the idea that I had money to spend. "You're American, aren't you?" asked an absolutely stunning blonde in a black-and-silver outfit that was smaller than those worn by the Los Angeles Raiders' cheerleaders.

"Yes," I responded, my eyes fighting a losing battle to stay focused on her face.

"Then it's like getting a discount, sweetie," she said in a starlet-to-movie-producer voice. "It's a hundred dollars Canadian, but if you pay in American dollars, it's only ninety." Glad as I was to see the American dollar making a comeback, I passed on her offer.

Back in my room I called the Pacific Hotel. They were holding my room reservation open. "I got tied up in San Francisco," I told the clerk. "I'll be there sometime tomorrow afternoon. Were there any messages for me?"

I could hear him shuffling papers. "Ah, just one, Mr. Polo. 'Welcome to Vancouver.' Signed, 'Raymond.'"

27

∎

"How's Vancouver?" Jane asked, as if she wasn't really all that interested.

"Beautiful city. Great food. And the prostitutes give you a discount for greenbacks."

"I hope you don't plan to bring home any unwanted souvenirs," she said dryly.

"Purely a matter of financial research," I assured her. "No sampling of the product. You don't sound too happy."

"I'm stuck in this damn hospital for another day. They want to take more x rays."

"How are you feeling?"

"Mad, sore, and hungry," she grumbled nastily. "What about your end? Any sight of Raymond?"

"No. I'm going boat-hunting this morning. If I don't have any luck there, I'll check into the Pacific Hotel and see what turns up."

"I still say you should call Jake Simpson."

"If I don't find the *Ramayana* today, I just may." I gave her the Harborside hotel's 800 number and my room number.

"Be careful, Nick." A pause. "I'm worried about you."

189

"Me too," I admitted.

I spent a couple of hours calling all the marinas and yacht clubs listed in the Vancouver telephone directory. None of them knew of the *Ramayana*. I put on all my armament, the Magnum in a shoulder holster, the .32 in an ankle holster, then went to the lobby and got some advice from the concierge. He recommended the Bayshore Yacht Harbor on Georgia, showing me on a map that it was within easy walking distance of the hotel.

The charter business appeared to be a little slow, so it didn't take long to find someone who suited my needs. "Johnstone," the tall man with the weather-beaten face said, holding out a calloused hand. "You can call me Boats." He was in his sixties and walked with the slight side-to-side motion that members of his calling develop over the years. He wore faded jeans, a heavy gray woolen sweater, and a navy-blue knit watch cap. The character played by Walter Brennan in the old Bogie flick loosely based on Hemingway's *To Have and Have Not* came to mind.

His boat was a sparkling-white Seaway express cruiser. "Usually I take out three or four people," Boats told me in a gravelly voice. "Got to charge you full price."

"I understand."

"And you don't want to do any fishing?"

"No. I'm looking for another boat." I gave him the description of the *Ramayana*.

"It's your money, mister," he said skeptically.

"Not anymore." I passed him three hundred-dollar bills.

He gave me a hard, probing look, one hand tugging at an earlobe. "You're carrying some pretty heavy cargo there, son." I opened my coat so that he could get a better look at the Magnum, then handed him one of my business cards.

"Private investigator," he said slowly, rubbing the card between his thumb and forefinger. "Is it as exciting in real life as it is in the books?"

"There are a lot more nymphomaniacs in the books," I answered truthfully.

He chuckled, then waved a sweatered arm toward his boat. "Welcome aboard."

Boats piloted his way directly over toward the Royal Vancouver Yacht Club, less than a mile from his own mooring. He expertly maneuvered the vessel through the yacht club's docks while I looked for anything resembling Regina's description of the *Ramayana*.

Boats went about his business. Then, once we were out in the harbor, he put the boat on automatic pilot, pulled two bottles of Corona beer from an ice chest, and tossed one to me. "Ain't none of my business, but I don't think you're going to have much luck finding this boat the way you're going at it."

I looked toward the shore and pointed out my hotel and the Sheraton. "I know it was in the water here and that a passenger could see the revolving roof of one of those hotels."

"How long ago was this?" Boats asked, after draining away half of his beer.

"A while back. But I think the boat is back up here. In Vancouver."

"Shit, son. Damn boat could be anywhere. Indian Arm, English Bay, out in the Georgia Strait, Howe Sound, any God-damn where. Thousand other places. You ain't got a chance."

I was beginning to believe him. I had been thinking along the lines of San Francisco Bay, which has a relatively small number of marinas that can handle a boat of the size that Regina had described: San Francisco itself, Sausalito, Alameda, a few more. But in Vancouver the possibilities were endless.

"Too bad you don't have a name for this boat of yours," Boats said, grabbing another beer from the ice chest before he took the wheel again.

"I do. The *Ramayana*. I called all the marinas listed in the directory, but no luck."

"Luck," Boats snorted, wiping foam from his lips with the back of his hand. "Luck never gets you nothing. Got to work for what you want." He looked at me over his shoulder. "Just how bad you want to find this here boat?"

"About three hundred more bucks' worth. Got any ideas?"

He smiled and spun the wheel, sending the boat into a long, lazy curve and cutting through the wake of a rusty tanker, the dark-green harbor waters foaming against its hull. "Sure do. Tell me what it looks like again."

"The person who described it doesn't know a lot about boats. But she said it was big. Very big. Several bedrooms and a big room like a living room, the main cabin, I guess. Black body, white sails, and windows. She was specific about the windows. They weren't portholes."

"How many people would this baby hold?" Boats said, idling the ship's twin motors back.

"Don't know for sure. Six, eight, ten, maybe more."

He gave me a wide grin, his teeth gleaming snow-white against his sunburned skin. "People like that, on a yacht, they got to eat. Got to drink. Probably like real fancy chow. Got to order it from somebody. Have it delivered, maybe. Boat that size needs supplies, servicing. You say it's got sails. I bet she's powered, too. Got to buy gas."

He coasted expertly to a stop, banging lightly into the old rubber-tire bumpers alongside his berth. "That's how you find a boat, mister," he said cutting the motors, then sprightly climbing onto the dock and fastening the mooring lines. "Wait here. Help yourself to the beer. There are sandwiches in the chest, too. I'll be back in a bit."

A bit turned out to be one Corona, two tunas on rye, and an hour and ten minutes later. Boats had a self-satisfied smile etched on his features as he made an awkward jump from the dock back onto his boat. "These people eat and drink pretty damn good, buddy. Pretty damn good. No jug wine on board that baby." He went to the wheelhouse, and the engines coughed to life. "The *Ramayana* is over at a club by Jericho Beach. Leastways she was yesterday."

We went back out into the water, passing under a span that Boats informed me was the Burraro Bridge. He turned south, and we hugged a rugged green coastline interrupted occasionally by sandy beaches until we came to the yacht club, a forest of tall masts, each boat looking slightly bigger and slightly more expensive-looking then its tied-up neighbor. There was no sign of the *Ramayana*.

Boats pulled into an area marked "guests," tied up, and went to talk to the harbormaster. He came back in a few minutes with that "I know something that you don't know" smile back on his face. "She's here, all right. Booked in for a couple of weeks. Must be out for a sail. Harbormaster says she's a real beauty. Worth looking at."

"I called all the yacht clubs and marinas listed in the yellow pages," I told him. "This place included. They told me they knew nothing about the *Ramayana*."

He scrunched his eyes up and spat into the lightly rolling dock waters. "Yacht club," he said, with the accent on the second word. "A club is what it is. You know, a fellow goes to a bar, and the bartender knows him, and this here fella's wife calls and asks for him, and the bartender tells her the fella, who's sitting right across from him, ain't there. You pay the kind of dock fees you have to pay here, and you tell the harbormaster you ain't here, then you ain't here. You know what I mean?"

"Yes, I know what you mean. But the harbormaster told you that the *Ramayana* was here."

"That's 'cause I told him I was here to do some work on her engines, son."

"Nice job. You should be a private eye."

Johnstone gave me a big smile. "Not enough nymphomaniacs."

We anchored off Jericho Beach and swapped sea stories. Boats was being slightly impressed by my teenage summers as a crab-pot fisherman in San Francisco. "That's hard work, son. Rough water, too." I had taken off my sport coat, stowing the Magnum in the cabin, out of sight. He gave me another hard look. "Still got some of those muscles you developed hauling up those pots, huh?"

"I'm glad I got something out of it," I admitted. Other than developing some muscles, the one thing I had taken away from those summers was a thorough knowledge of hard, backbreaking work, something I had been trying to avoid ever since. Fourteen hours a day in the rolling Pacific Ocean on those small wooden one-cylinder boats that the tourists thought were so picturesque had cured me of any ideas that I might have had about of the romance of the sea. Boats Johnstone's life had been just the opposite. He had joined the U.S. Navy at seventeen and had lived on or near saltwater ever since.

193

The ice chest was out of food and low on beer by the time Boats spotted the big, black-hulled yacht. "Goddamn, she's something. Take a look." He handed me a pair of navy-style Bausch and Lomb binoculars. The vessel was extremely broad for a sailing ship and well over a hundred feet in length, the tip of the mainmast appearing even longer than the ship itself. The sails were down, and she was purring along at a good clip under power. The big windows that Regina had been so sure about were there, all right, strung along the boat's side and giving it a somewhat awkward look. I could make out the gold scroll on the hull: *Ramayana*.

There were three people on deck, bundled up in brightly colored windbreakers. The man behind the wheel was Gurbeep Singh. I could see him smile, then say something to a dark-haired youth in his twenties. He patted the younger man's shoulder and turned the wheel over to him. The third person was Marta Howard, stretched out in a deck chair, long legs traveling up to yellow shorts and a white turtleneck. Gurbeep opened his mouth and then gestured toward her. She tipped up her sunglasses, dropped a magazine to the deck, and joined him as they disappeared belowdeck.

28

■

I found a stationery store, bought a dozen large manila envelopes and a tube of superglue, then went back to my hotel, stopping at the restaurant in the lobby to scoop up a handful of matchbooks. Once back in my room, I went to work on some of the envelopes, glueing the matchbook strikers and the matches in their proper position. When an envelope was opened, contact was made, and a spark erupted from the match. I didn't need a flame, just a spark. After a few tries I was reasonably sure I had it right. Reasonably sure isn't really good enough when your life may depend on it, but it was as good as I was going to get.

I then worked on a final model, and when I was satisfied I slipped in twenty sheets of flash paper, the stuff that magicians used onstage, ordinary bond paper that has been impregnated with a high-potassium black-powder compound. Though it's available in most magic shops, the number-one customers are not magicians but bookies, who use it to jot down their bets while keeping a lighted candle or butane lighter within easy reach in case they hear a symphony of flat feet pounding up the steps. Poof, the evidence is gone. So is the bookie, if he's not careful.

I stuffed another manila envelope with plain hotel stationery, packed my suitcase, slipping the harmless manila envelope into one of the bag's outer zippered pockets, then walked over to the Pacific Hotel. My reservation was waiting. "Room Eleven-forty-two," the efficient clerk told me, and then went on to extol the hotel's amenities: a sauna, a whirlpool, a steam room, a tennis court, a racquetball court, a tanning room, a massage room, and its own jogging track. He also informed me that the room rate was $320 a night. Expensive, but then there was that American-dollar-to-Canadian-dollar discount that the hooker had enlightened me about.

The clerk's professional smile drooped a bit when I told him that eleven was an unlucky number for me. He played with his computer, fingers flying over the keys as fast as Harry Connick, Jr.'s, do while playing an Ellington melody on the piano. "How would room Twelve-eighteen be, sir?" he asked.

"Just fine. I'd like to put something in the hotel safe," I told him, making a production of unzipping my luggage and handing him the harmless manila envelope. "Be careful with that, please," I advised him in a loud voice. "There are some very important documents inside."

A uniformed bellman grabbed my bag and led me to the elevators. There was no sign of the Singh gang, but the lobby was jammed and was big enough to hide the *Ramayana*, if Gurbeep could find a way to skipper the boat in from the nearby waterfront.

The suite was beautifully decorated and looked right out onto Vancouver Harbor. I searched around for a spot for the manila envelope with the flash paper, finally settling for an old standby, under the cushion of a padded chair near the sliding glass doors leading to a small sundeck.

I showered, putting the Magnum on a towel within arm's reach, shaved, dressed, then rang room service for dinner: steak, salad, baked potato, apple pie, iced tea. While working my way through the meal, it dawned on me that it resembled what a condemned man might order while waiting for that last reprieve from the governor.

All that beer with Boats Johnstone had taken away my

appetite, so the plates were still half-filled when I placed them outside the door. I turned the television on and waited to see who Singh would send. There was a movie in which Roddy McDowell was rambling around a haunted house. I didn't pay much attention to it. From what I did see, neither had McDowell.

It was a little after ten when the phone rang. "Hi. I'd like to talk," purred the sexy voice of Marta Howard. "But you have to promise you won't run away this time."

"Who's with you, Marta?"

"No one. Not even Jasmine. My, my. You don't know how much fun you missed that night, Nick. Are you going to let me come up?"

"Sure. Room Twelve-eighteen."

There was a light tapping on the door a few minutes later. "Come on in. It's open," I yelled from across the room, the Magnum pointed at the center of the door.

It's always better to leave the door unlocked in a situation like that, rather than creep up, gun in hand, lean over, open the door, and jump back the way they do in the movies. Someone on the other side of that door could have one of those semi-automatic, machine-gun-type pistols that squirrel hunters always protest about when they're about to be banned, and could let loose a deadly spray in a pattern several yards wide, penetrating the door, the walls, and our poor gun-in-hand hero.

Marta Howard strode in confidently. All that seaside fresh air had given her a nice tan. Her hair was pulled back at the sides and coiled into a twist. That part of her hair looked slightly different shade of blond from the rest. It also looked like a lot more hair than she'd had when I'd last seen her. She was wearing a lemon-yellow tank dress, cinched at the waist with a wide beige leather belt. A yellow cardigan hung loosely on her shoulders. Her purse's leather matched the belt.

"Close the door behind you," I ordered, waving the gun at her.

"Sure," she said cheerfully, swiveling around and pushing the door closed. Then peeked over her shoulder and said, "I guess you want it locked, too."

197

"You guess right," I said, moving toward the bed. "Toss your purse over here."

She heaved it my way. I let it hit the floor, then bent over to pick it up, spilling the contents onto the bedspread: tubes of lipstick; a compact; keys; cigarettes; a heavy gold lighter; tissues; Binaca; a healthy roll of fifties, twenties, and a few ones held together by a heart-shaped money clip; and some coins, both American and Canadian. I examined each item before replacing it in the purse, which I then threw toward the couch.

"Disappointed?" Marta called to me. "I wouldn't want you to think I'm hiding anything, Nick." She shrugged the cardigan off her shoulders and undid the belt buckle, then slowly pulled her dress over her shoulders. She narrowed her eyes, put her hands on her hips, and pushed her shoulders back, causing her breasts to jut upward. She wasn't wearing a bra, and her swimsuit had protected just an inch or so of white skin from the sun's rays. Nylon stockings climbed up her long legs, stopping at midthigh all by themselves, with nothing to hold them up. I'd have to tell Jane about that. Then she could get rid of the garter belt that swine Roy had given her.

"Not satisfied yet?" Marta questioned, then hooked her thumbs into the sides of her brief white bikini panties and wiggled her way out of them. "Now are you satisfied?" she asked, swaying elegantly on her high heels.

"Almost," I said, pointing the barrel of the gun toward the bed. "Come on over here."

She jiggled over confidently, her lips curled in a smirk, perching on the end of the bed, stretching those long legs out in front of her, crossing her arms under her breasts so they pointed up at me like twin minirockets.

"Let your hair down," I said.

She pursed her lips, then gave me that smile again. I wondered whether she'd practiced in front of a mirror to get it just that way or whether it came naturally. She patted the mattress with her right hand. "It's better up and out of the way, Nicky. I want you to watch my face when I make love to you."

"Undo it, Marta."

198

She rose to her feet. "Just let me use the bathroom for a minute, darling, and—"

I pushed her roughly back to the bed. "Undo it. Now."

Her hands went reluctantly to the back of her head, fiddling away, her eyes boring into mine all the while, her tongue snaking out over those wet red lips.

"Quit stalling, Marta," I said, surprised at the hoarseness of my voice.

She pulled out a long hatpin. Very long. And thicker than what was needed to hold the blond hairpiece, which came loose and fell to the bed. I motioned her away, picked up the hairpiece and shook it out, as if it were a dirty dust mop. Two miniature syringes filled with a clear liquid fell out, landing noiselessly on the floor.

Marta had slid to the far end of the bed, holding the hairpin in her hand as if it were a switchblade knife. "Stick the pin into the bed, Marta. All the way in." The smirk on her face had turned into a snarl, and she let out a string of curses as she jammed the pin into the bedspread.

"Now lie down. Face down. Spread those arms and legs."

A look of confusion crossed her features. She twisted her neck, her eyes following me as I picked up her belt. "Hands behind your back, sexy." There was more than confusion in those eyes now. Fear, mixed with excitement. She joined her hands together and I looped the belt around them several times, tying the ends off in a square knot.

Marta rolled over to her side, her upper teeth biting into her lower lip. "That's so tight, Nick," she whispered, her whole body shuddering. "So tight. I like it like that."

I bent down and carefully picked up one of the syringes. "We're not playing any of your S and M games, Marta, darling." I tested the syringe. A little line of the clear liquid squirted out from the end of the needle. "I hope what you have in here isn't lethal, kid." I ran a hand over her buttocks.

"You bastard! You prick! You no-good son of a—" She screamed when the needle pricked her skin.

"Is it lethal, Marta? Because if it is, you're going to die." Luckily, she took my threat seriously. If she had said that what-

199

ever was in the damn syringe could kill, I'd never have performed the nasty deed. But when she said that it would just put someone to sleep, I jammed the needle in all the way and squeezed the syringe's handle.

She began lashing out with her legs, and I got a lot more "You bastard! You prick!" dialogue, along with some additional salty language that would have curled what was left of the hair on Boats Johnstone's head.

I held the other syringe in front of her face. "Calm down, or you'll get this one in your other cheek."

She was rocking up and down, her face buried in the spread, still cursing, but the volume going down several decibels every second. When she was still, I bent my head close to hers. "Who else is here in the hotel, Marta?" She spat at me, just missing, but it wasn't a bad try considering her position and condition.

I waved the syringe in front of her face, like a stage hypnotist waving a prop. "Who else is here?" I repeated. The chemicals in the syringe were doing the job they'd been designed for. Her breathing was slowing down, her eyeballs rolling upward. All of a sudden she was out.

I took the second syringe to the bathroom, squirted the contents into the toilet bowl, and dumped the syringe into the wastebasket. Marta was snoring deeply when I got back to the bed. I undid the belt, put a pillow under her head, and flipped the bedspread over so that it covered her from shoulder to toes.

One down. How many to go? Someone was out there waiting. Pirate Beard or a few just like him. I wondered what their plan was. Marta had come in loaded for bear. Bare bear, in fact. The hatpin could have done serious damage. And if one of those syringes could put her out in a matter of seconds, what would two have done to me?

And what were they planning to do with me if she'd been successful? I walked to the sliding doors, pulled them back, and peered over the balcony railing. Twelve floors. Nothing below but cement and some parked cars. I shuddered, then went back inside the room. How long would Marta Howard's playmates give her to get the job done? They would have a definite timetable, with alternative plans if I somehow failed to succumb to her charms.

I decided to send a signal of my own, calling room service and ordering a bottle of champagne, with a promise of a ten-dollar tip if they got it to me in under five minutes. I retrieved the manila envelope from its hiding place and slipped it under my shirt. Ah, the power of incentives. He beat the mark by almost a full minute. A knock on the door, then the call "Room service."

"It's open." This time I kept the Magnum in its holster, under my jacket, my hand on the butt, my finger on the trigger.

A youngster barely out of his teens, with a big smile, came in carrying a tray that held a champagne bottle nestled in a plastic ice bucket and two fluted glasses.

His eyes strayed to the bed, his ears picking up Marta's sonorous symphony. I shrugged my shoulders, signed the chit, and handed him an American ten-spot. "Is there an ice machine on this floor?" I asked him.

"Yes, sir. Down at the end of the hallway, just before the stairs." He set the bucket down on a small, round table near the sliding glass doors. "But the champagne is cold, sir. I made sure of that."

"I'm sure you did, son. It's just that my wife has a craving for ice sometimes. Maybe you can show me just where the machine is."

I made a brief stop at the bathroom, picking up an empty ice bucket identical to the one from room service. We exited the room together, the kid asking me whether I was enjoying my stay, where I was from, normal hotel chitchat.

The doorway marked "Stairs" was under a red exit light. The door was slightly ajar. I kept talking to the kid, who stopped at the elevator and pushed the down button. I was in luck. Within seconds there was a ping and the elevator doors hissed open. There were a half-dozen people in the elevator, all of them normal, happy, vacationing-tourist-type people. I joined them, holding my empty bucket in front of my stomach, my right hand slipped inside my sport coat, Napoleon style. In those portraits of Mr. Bonaparte, with his hand under his tunic, he always seemed to me to be suppressing a grin. As my finger moved gently up and down the Magnum's trigger, I wondered just what the late, lamented emperor of France had been fondling under there.

29

∎

My luck was holding. The elevator dropped all the way to the lobby level without any stops in between. My fellow passengers exited for whatever late-night pleasures they had in mind. I hugged the walls, picking up a sawed-off view of the lobby area, then pushed the button to go down one floor to the hotel garage.

If someone had been waiting behind that door on the twelfth floor, he would still be running down those stairs after me. But if he had some type of walkie-talkie, he could have called in to his comrades and there would be a reception committee waiting for me. Big ifs, but under the circumstances, ifs I had to worry about.

There were two men waiting for the elevator when I got to the garage level. Both were in their mid-to-late thirties, and both were wearing glasses and business suits. They paid me no attention as I brushed by them, sprinting into a line of parked cars. I followed the yellow arrows on the cement floor up a concrete ramp and out onto the street.

The weather had turned cold. A sharp, icy wind was blowing discarded trash down the street. Leaves crunched under my shoes as I ran in a serpentine path for a couple of blocks, flagging down a cab that had just dropped people at a waterfront restaurant.

"Jericho Bay Yacht Club," I told the driver, through deep gasps for more oxygen. There's something about running away from people who mean you bodily harm that tends to suck you dry. I hadn't seen anyone following, but I still didn't think there was much of a possibility that Gurbeep would have sent Marta to me without a backup team. I was hoping for a small window of opportunity while the bad guys were busy trying to wake up Marta and figure out where I'd gone to. Just a half-hour or so when the *Ramayana* might be vulnerable.

I leaned forward and handed the cab driver a five-dollar bill. "I'm in a hurry," I told him. He merely nodded his head and snatched the bill away from me. I settled back into the cab's imitation-leather seats, then immediately bounced forward again. "You happen to have a flashlight?"

"Sure." He reached out and patted a hand on the dashboard. "In the glove compartment. You need it now?"

I passed him a twenty-dollar bill this time. "I'd like to buy it."

The Jericho Bay Yacht Club was having some type of party in its clubhouse, a four-story white batten-board building with terra-cotta-colored wooden shingles that looked as if it had spent its earlier life as a lighthouse. A brass railing led up the front steps.

A gentleman with a white tuxedo jacket held up a hand as I was about to enter. "I'm with Charles," I told him brusquely, figuring that a club like this had to have at least one Charles on the preferred membership roll, and elbowed my way in among the well-dressed throng.

I skirted the dance floor, which was jammed with more tuxedo jackets leading pleasant-faced women in evening gowns around the floor to the beat of a hardworking, five-piece band playing a soft version of "Green Dolphin Street," an appropriate tune considering the setting.

I found an exit by the bar that led to the boat moorings. It was a first-class yacht club, no rotting wooden piers here. The scrubbed cement walkways were lined with a ribbon of coconut-fiber matting. Each boat slip had a neatly coiled length of rubber hose in front of it. I went to the slip where Boats Johnstone and I had watched the *Ramayana* dock earlier in the afternoon. The boat was still there.

There was a ribbon of colored Chinese lanterns on the wooden railing leading to the boat. The matting muffled my footsteps. I had the cabbie's flashlight in one hand, the Magnum in the other. There were lights coming from two of the boat's windows, but I couldn't hear anything, other than the water lapping on the dock and the bonelike creaking of nearby boats as they bobbed gently up and down, straining against their mooring lines.

A brightly painted white wooden gangplank lead up to the *Ramayana*'s teak deck. I went up it slowly, like a tightrope walker, one foot at a time, stopping with every step, closing my eyes briefly, concentrating on the sounds nearby. I sprayed the flashlight around the deck. Nothing there looked out of place. No Sinbad the Sailor types crouched behind the masts, knives between gleaming teeth, waiting to pounce.

Directly in front of the boat's wheel was an open hatch leading "below," as they like to say in yachting circles. Little brass light fixtures in the shape of ship's bells led the way below. There were no narrow vertical ladders on this baby. The steps were some five feet in width and covered with beige carpeting that matched the wall paneling.

The huge room created the feeling that you were in an upscale apartment rather than a yacht. Three Tiffany-style lamps cast puddles of light around the room. The ceiling was as high as in a house, a good eight feet. The large, rectangular windows gazed out onto the black waters of English Bay. Picasso prints hung from the walls. The chocolate-brown couch was deep and comfortable-looking. The four chairs surrounding the dining table were good-sized, with leather basket-weave backs. There was a built-in bar alongside the far wall. On the bar were several photographs in silver frames, all of the *Ramayana* under full sail. I fingered one of the frames, looking around the room and thinking of the acts that Regina and her little chums had been forced to perform in this very room.

205

An open archway led to a corridor lined with five doors, two on one side, three on the other. I pressed my ear to the first of the doors, then turned the knob slowly. Apparently Gurbeep wasn't worried about his electric bill. Both bedside lamps were on. The king-sized bed dominated the room. Floor-length drapes partially covered the eye-height windows. I paced it off. Fourteen by twenty. Not many ocean liners had suites that size. The *Ramayana* seemed to be a boat built for someone who didn't want to wake up knowing he was on a boat. A shutter-door closet took up one wall. Inside were rows of neatly hung clothing: men's suits, tuxedoes, sport coats, slacks. Clear lucite drawers showed a rainbow of sweaters and shirts.

I went back to the hallway and checked the other rooms, pressing my ear against each mahogany door before carefully turning the lock and peering in. More bedrooms, not as large or as nicely furnished as the master suite, but still not bad. One had twin bunks, both a tangle of twisted sheets and blankets. There were dirty clothes in piles on the floor. I used a toe to disturb one of the piles: men's pants, shirts, and underwear. It suddenly reminded me of the condition of the bedrooms in the house at 25 the Holtons, in London.

The adjoining room reeked of perfume, and the women's clothes were all sleek and expensive-looking, the kind Marta Howard wore. The next door lead to what looked like a vacant motel room: neatly made-up bed, empty closet and dresser drawers.

When I pressed my ear to the last door I could hear soft moaning, then silence, then a voice mumbling something I couldn't understand. The voice sounded young. Very young. I tried the doorknob. The door was locked. I tapped lightly on the door paneling with the butt of the Magnum. There was no response other than more of the moaning and mumbling sounds. I knocked harder with the gun butt. Still there was no response.

There were a chrome fire extinguisher and a fire ax fastened to the wall at the far end of the hallway. I grabbed the ax. The handle was bare wood, the working end painted fire-engine red. It looked as if it had never seen action before. I edged the ax blade into the small gap between the door and the wall molding and leaned against the handle. There was a loud crack as the door popped open. I moved inside, waving the ax like a Viking about to do a little plundering.

There were two twin beds. On top of each was a small, dark-haired child. They looked about four years of age. Both were asleep. I couldn't tell whether they were boys or girls. The one on the right was moaning and wriggling against the strap that bound him to the bed. The other was deep in sleep, eyes squeezed shut, little forehead wrinkled as if in pain.

The straps were nylon, much like the material used on seat belts. One end was tied to the bed frame, then wrapped around the child's body several times. The other end was tied off on the opposite side of the bed in a knot I remembered from my crab-fishing days as a clove hitch. I undid the knot on each bed, keeping my eyes on the children. They looked so small, so vulnerable, so frightened, even in sleep. It must have been a drugged sleep. Neither responded to me when I tried to shake them awake.

They were both wearing identical flannel pajamas, in a Walt Disney print: Mickey, Donald, Pluto, Goofy, all the favorites were cavorting around with happy grins on their faces. The pajamas were damp with sweat. I hoisted one child over my left shoulder, then struggled to get the other in position over my right shoulder. They were both heavier than they looked, dead weight. But at least they were breathing. The one over my right shoulder started struggling a bit, then crying. I looked at the taut, frightened little face and swore.

It was time to get out of there, time to call in Jake Simpson at the INS and every available cop in Vancouver. I moved as fast as I could but had to be careful going through the door frame so that I didn't bump my passenger's heads. As much as I would have liked to have the Magnum available, I needed both hands to keep the kids from slipping off my shoulders. I was out of the hall, into the main saloon, and halfway up the stairs to the outer deck.

Maybe it was the child's moaning. Maybe it was the rage ringing in my ears. Maybe it was the fact that I was calling Gurbeep Singh every rotten word I could think of. Maybe I was just stupid. Whatever the reason, I hadn't heard them come on board. They were waiting for me on the top step: Gurbeep in a shiny blue suit, Pirate Beard holding a long-barreled automatic, and Hardev Singh with his Philippine butterfly knife in his hand.

"You keep breaking into my property and stealing my valuable belongings, Mr. Polo," Gurbeep Singh said, his voice flat, completely devoid of expression. "We are going to have to put a stop to that."

30

∎

I backed down slowly, the weight of the children on my shoulders seeming to double. "Hardev," Gurbeep Singh barked out. "Relieve Mr. Polo of his burden." He turned toward Pirate Beard. "Darshan, if he makes even the slightest effort to resist, shoot him. Be careful not to hit the boys."

Hardev took the child from my left shoulder and dumped him on the chocolate-brown couch as if he were a sack of potatoes. He ran the flat side of his knife blade across my cheek before snatching the other boy, again tossing him on the couch as if he were anything but a human being.

I looked at Pirate Beard. Gurbeep had called him Darshan, not the name I would have picked. His jaw muscles were working overtime, and a vein was throbbing directly in the middle of his forehead.

"You are a troublesome man, Mr. Polo," Gurbeep said, reaching inside his suit jacket for a leather cigar case. He rolled the cigar in his hand and snipped off the end with his teeth, spitting the small piece of tobacco to the floor. He took his time getting the thing lit, then tilted his head to one side to keep the smoke out of his eyes and continued: "Troublesome indeed. Resourceful, I must admit. But troublesome."

Pirate Beard rattled off some Hindi at him. Gurbeep smiled. "Darshan said that you treated him poorly at the farm. He is anxious to 'get even,' as you Americans call it." His smile deepened. "Usually Darshan prefers young boys like those." He waved a hand toward the couch. "But in your case he will make an exception."

"I thought we had a deal," I said. "I've got those computer printouts. From the farm in Yuba City. The assessor records list all that property under the names of some people called Sidhu. More cousins? Or just another name you like to use?"

If my intent was to rattle Gurbeep, I wasn't having much success. He took a long draw on his cigar, then said: "What's in a name, Mr. Polo? When you or some nosy police agency gets too close, I just choose another one."

Hardev was back with his knife. This time he ran the edge down my cheek. I could feel the blood spurt out and roll down my neck. Hardev started to pat me down. Finding the Magnum, he pulled it roughly from its holster and smacked me across the nose with the barrel.

Pirate Beard was getting excited. He said something to Gurbeep. "Yes," Gurbeep responded. "A good idea. Darshan wants you to take off your clothes, Mr. Polo. Like you made him do. Only he wants you to strip naked. Too bad Marta isn't here. She'd enjoy watching this."

Pirate Beard stepped forward and jabbed his gun barrel into my stomach. "Strip," he shouted in English, grabbing my sportcoat sleeve and yanking it so hard I almost fell to the floor. I struggled out of the coat, then began undoing the holster straps.

"What about those computer printouts?" I asked Gurbeep again.

He leaned his head back and blew a perfect smoke ring at the ceiling. "A bad move on your part, Mr. Polo. There is no possible way you could have gained entrance to those files. No possible way you could know the passwords."

"Are you sure? I found the *Ramayana*."

He took the cigar from his mouth and compressed his bloodless lips. "Yes. I did agree you were resourceful. I'm interested in just how you did learn about the *Ramayana*. I'm sure that Hardev and Darshan can get you to tell us all about it. If you had told the police, they'd be with you now. No, I'm afraid those papers you so diligently placed in the hotel's safe are completely worthless. Completely."

"You might think so," I said. "But not the INS. Or the London cops. They've got you in mind for the murder of your clerk, Ronnie. Judging from the knife wound I saw, Hardev must have done the dirty work. Why kill a harmless clerk like that? You screwed up there."

"Perhaps," he said indifferently. He drew on his cigar again, then said: "Ronald was becoming a problem. Too inquisitive. I can thank you for pointing that out when you found me at Blackwell's casino. You told me that you had been to the shop and given him a copy of Raymond's check. Ronald never mentioned it to us. Not until Hardev interrogated him. Yes, you did me a real favor there. Hardev was able to persuade Ronald to tell us quite a bit. He was much like you, Mr. Polo. Delusions of grandeur. He thought he could blackmail me. He knew something wasn't quite on the up and up at BeeJay's. He'd been keeping notes. Foolish man. It is a shame to lose the store. It made a nice front for our trips to India."

I can imagine those trips: Marta Howard buying schlock for the racks at BeeJay's while Gurbeep and Hardev went child-shopping. Pirate Beard was gesturing at me with his gun barrel to get on with the striptease.

"I didn't put all the papers in the safe." I tapped my chest. "I've got half of them here. Along with the photographs. I had them cropped and enlarged. They're very clear. You, Marta, Raymond. Where is Raymond?"

Gurbeep nodded his head at Hardev, who ripped open my shirt and pulled the manila envelope from my waistband. He handed it to Gurbeep, who balanced it in one hand as if he were trying to guess its weight. "Poor Raymond," Gurbeep said. "Did you know he was a terrible swimmer? Of course, it could have been the anchor he was tied to that dragged him down." Gurbeep's mouth approximated a smile. "Raymond was a foolish man. We were close once. Business partners in some boring

211

real-estate deals. Then he began sticking his nose in where it did not belong."

"Maybe he didn't like what you and your playmates were doing to his relatives, like the boys over there," I said, my eyes on the manila envelope. "That's what the check I delivered was for, wasn't it? The safe delivery of the two children?"

"Yes, but not those two. His precious little cousins are still in the pipeline." Gurbeep waved a hand in the air. "Foolish man. That tape you delivered to me was full of threats. Raymond did not understand the ways of the world." He pointed the tip of his cigar at the couch. "Do you really think those two unfortunate creatures would be better off at home? Living like animals. No protection from hunger or disease." He moved his head from side to side. "No. They will be much better off when I place them with the right people."

"Did you ever think of asking them whether that's what they want?"

Gurbeep bared his white teeth in frustration. "Fool. You're a stupid fool. Like Raymond. And you'll suffer the same fate, I'm afraid." He swiveled on his heel and looked as if he were going to walk up the stairs leading to the deck.

"Those pictures," I called to his back. "I've had copies made. They'll be sent to the police."

He turned back slowly, a look of superiority on his face. "Another empty threat," he said. "So you have pictures of Raymond and me and Marta. So what?"

"The pictures show your airplane and Raymond being dragged on board. The police will be interested in those pictures. Believe me. His family has already filed a missing-persons report."

I don't know whether he believed me, but he was interested enough to open the manila envelope. I was holding my breath and could swear that I heard the scratching of the match just before the sheets of flash paper ignited, sending out an instant high-temperature flame with a radius of some five feet. Gurbeep screamed as the fire licked at his face and clothing.

I dropped to one knee, rolling toward the couch, my hand grasping for the .32 revolver in its ankle holster. Both Pirate

Beard and Hardev ran to help Gurbeep, who was running blindly, crashing into the wall. The flash paper had dropped to the carpet, the flames leaping to the window curtains.

I had the revolver in my hand by the time Pirate Beard remembered me. I fired three quick rounds at him from a distance of eight or nine feet. Even I couldn't miss at that range. He managed to squeeze off one shot as he fell to the carpet. A searing pain shot through my left arm. Hardev ran at me, knife in hand, his face a gargoyle of rage. His face registered shock as my first shot hit him in the stomach. He kept coming, his right arm going back as if getting ready to throw the knife. I shot him again and continued pulling the trigger even after I heard nothing but the metal click of an empty gun.

Gurbeep was rolling on the floor, trying to smother the fire burning at his clothing and flesh. I reached for a bottle of vodka on the bar, smashed the bottom of the bottle against the edge of the bar rail, and hurled it at him. The alcohol erupted, the flames flashing a bright blue, then a glowing orange. Gurbeep struggled to his feet, arms outstretched, spinning out of control like a child's top losing its momentum, inhuman sounds spouting from the blackening hole that was his mouth.

My left arm was useless, and for a moment I panicked. The smoke was getting thick. It was hard to breathe. The drapes were completely engulfed in flames, and the toxic smell of the burning carpet seared my lungs. I wanted to bolt up those stairs. I dropped to my knees, crawled to the couch, and managed to get one of the children over my left shoulder. I grabbed the second boy, hugged him to my chest, and got up slowly, afraid that the one on my shoulder would slip off at any second.

I skirted what was left of Gurbeep and made it to the stairs. The fresh air gave me a second wind, and I was off the boat and onto the dock before my legs gave out. I lay there, panting for breath, watching the flames spread through the *Ramayana*, my good arm encircling the two boys. I don't know how long we lay there on the dock. Probably just a minute or two. My left arm was aching badly, and try as I might to get to my feet, I just couldn't do it.

I must have passed out for a moment, because all of a

sudden I found myself surrounded by gleaming leather shoes. A white-haired gentleman bent down and began exploring my arm. "Relax," he said. "I'm a doctor. We'd better move you, get you to a hospital. That damn boat might just blow up." He gestured toward the two boys. "These your kids?"

"Damn right," I said. "Goddamn right."

There were two uniformed officers waiting at the hospital. Both middle-aged veterans with bored looks on their faces. They followed me from the ambulance to surgery and then to my room. They didn't say much, answering all my questions with noncommittal grunts.

You can usually tell what kind of a cop a person is by the way his fellow cops treat him. When a young, good-looking, dark-haired guy in a gray suit came in, both cops greeted him good-naturedly.

"Hey, Benny," one said. "When can I get sprung from here? I've got police work to do."

"Yeah," the other piped in. "Besides, we missed our dinner break."

Gray suit nodded and smiled. "Take a hike. You're both useless anyway." He came alongside the bed, reached into his suit pocket, and gave me a quick look at his badge. "Lieutenant Jetson, Polo. You ready to tell me what the hell went on down at the yacht club?"

It was one of those snap decisions. Jetson just looked like a cop who not only knew the rules but also knew how to play the game. Besides, I didn't have much choice. I gave him the whole story. After a half-hour of my rambling yarn, Jetson held up a hand. "I want to get a stenographer in here, Polo. Any objection?"

"No. How are the two kids?"

"Your sons?" he inquired with a small smile. "Okay, I guess. After what you've told me, I'd better get the sexual-trauma team up here. Looks like they've had a tough time."

"What about the boat?" I asked. "Anyone on board still alive?"

"By the time the fire department got there it was pretty well

214

gone. It's going to take a hell of a lot of work by the coroner to identify the three bodies," Jetson said. He stood up, ran a hand down his tie, and squinted at me. "From what you said, it doesn't sound like a great loss."

"I don't want to tell you your job, Lieutenant, but it might be a good idea to get ahold of Jake Simpson at the INS. Have him get to that farm in Yuba City, California, and see whether that computer is still there. If some technicians can get the information out of that hard disk, they may come up with Gurbeep Singh's client list. No telling how many more kids he's sold."

"Yeah, yeah, yeah," Jetson said, heading for the door. He went out, then came right back, holding the door open with one hand. "Anybody back home you want notified, Polo?"

I gave him Jane's name and phone number. He wrote the information down in a notebook, took a quick peek out in the hallway, then said softly: "Get to sleep. I'll be back in the morning with the stenographer." He surprised me by giving me a big wink with his right eye. "Looks like you done good, Polo. But you'd better have an attorney at bedside when I come back in the morning."

31
.

"People are staring," I told Jane Tobin.

She glanced around the room. "Well, we do look pretty silly, don't we?"

We were sitting in the dining room of the restaurant at the Basque Cultural Center, a jewel nestled among the industrial buildings and abandoned railroad tracks in South San Francisco. At one time it was relatively unknown, except to its many regulars, who kept the information about the fantastic food and reasonable prices to themselves to keep the crowds away. A rave review in the local paper had lifted the veil of secrecy, and now the place was jammed every night.

If we had ordered fish it wouldn't have been much of a problem, but since Jane wanted the rack of lamb and I was in the mood for pepper steak, we had to work as a team. Jane would hold the fork on my steak with her one good hand, and I'd saw off a few bites. Then I'd return the compliment, sticking my fork into her lamb while she cut into the juicy pink meat. Louis, the dapper maître d', had taken one look at us, Jane's left arm in a cast, mine in a sling, and suggested that we might enjoy sitting side by side rather than across from each other.

I dabbed a piece of the thick steak into the cognac sauce. Jane was casting admiring looks at my plate, so I was in a bit of a rush to get down as much of the steak as possible before she gave me her "Gee, I'm starving" look. "Will you have to go back to Vancouver, Nick?" she asked.

"Yes. Lieutenant Jetson wants me there day after tomorrow for the inquest."

"He sounds like a nice guy."

"He is," I said. "Nice, and sharp. He and Jake Simpson get along well."

Jane abandoned our routine with the knife and fork and picked up her lamb by the bone. I topped off our wineglasses, wondering whether I could get away with the same thing on my steak.

"What about the children?" Jane asked. "What will happen to them?"

"Simpson wasn't sure. They'll be undergoing therapy for a while."

"I hope poor Regina and her mother aren't in any trouble."

"Me too," I agreed, "but I don't know. Raymond Singh's wife's attorney called me at the hospital. Jetson had told her the news about Raymond. I hinted to the attorney that I would be a lot more cooperative if Regina and her mother were given something, maybe a piece of the store. The attorney wants a signed declaration that I heard Gurbeep say that they buried Raymond at sea. So maybe we've got a little leverage there."

Jane pushed her plate away and stared at mine longingly. We compromised, going back to our knife-and-fork act and splitting the remains of the pepper steak. "God," she said with a sigh when the plate was wiped clean, "if we have this much trouble eating, how are we ever going to make love?"

"Carefully," I crooned into her ear. "Very carefully."